His lips were against hers, hard and commanding.

What happened next shocked them both. Annabelle's body seemed to leap into flame. His hand slid up her back to caress her neck under the heavy weight of her tumbling hair.

And then a little sharp cold thought entered his brain. He had no intention of seducing Annabelle Carruthers or becoming involved in any messy liaison. He stood up abruptly and said in a husky voice, "It is late."

Annabelle watched, wide-eyed, as he strode from the room.

Damn the man! He was a devil to arouse her so. Now she was really frightened of him. . . .

HIS LORDSHIP'S PLEASURE

Marion Chesney

FAWCETT CREST • NEW YORK

A Fawcett Crest Book
Published by Ballantine Books
Copyright © 1991 by Marion Chesney

Library of Congress Catalog Card Number: 91-91817

ISBN 0-449-21763-9

Manufactured in the United States of America

First Edition: May 1991

Chapter One

ANNABELLE, MRS. CARRUTHERS, walked down the drive of the Manor House, her heart as heavy as lead. In London the Season was about to begin and she would miss it all because her husband had had to flee from town pursued by his many debtors. He must rusticate, he had said, and of course that rustication included his wife.

She did not pine for the balls and parties of the Season, but for the company of her two friends, Matilda, Duchess of Hadshire, and Emma, Comtesse Saint Juste. Emma perhaps might not wish to see her, for before her happy marriage to the comte, Emma had been abducted by her first husband's murderers, traitors working for the French, and Annabelle feared her husband had taken money from the criminals to assist in that abduction, although he still swore his innocence when he was sober enough to do so. But Matilda would be there; Matilda, who was as unhappily married as Annabelle and therefore a great source of comfort.

Annabelle felt very alone. Such servants as they were able to afford were rough and uncouth. She had no lady's maid and her husband's reputation was so bad that no member of the local gentry came to call. The vicar had made a brave visit but had had the port decanter thrown at his head for his pains.

Guy Carruthers had been gambling again and she had gone through his pockets that morning while he slept and removed a few shillings. She was on her way to the mercers in the village of Upper Chipping to buy silk ribbon to refurbish one of her old gowns. The high Cotswold hedges were full of bird song as she let herself out through the large iron gates of the manor beside the deserted lodge and walked down the lane that led to the village. The sky was pale blue and there was warmth in the southerly wind and green buds on the boughs of the trees. Water chuckled in the ditch beside the road and a curious blackbird eyed her suspiciously as if wondering how anyone could look so miserable on such a glorious day.

And Annabelle *was* miserable. She had lost all hope of ever seeing her marriage recover from the bitter drunken depths to which it had sunk. She found herself hating her husband and dreamt longingly of his death, at the same time finding these evil thoughts frightening, as if she could wish him to death.

She was a tall woman in her early twenties dressed in good but shabby clothes. She had rich brown curly hair and large gray eyes. Her figure was deep bosomed and her waist trim. Her mouth was large and generous, a sad fault in an age where beauty demanded a small, pouting rosebud mouth, but hers was a mouth made for love and laughter and when she was in good spirits—although that was an increasingly rare event—she was extremely attractive.

Outside the village, she passed the high gates and walls of the Darkwood estates. She had heard the servants talking about the return of the wicked Earl of Darkwood from the wars. He seemed to have caused great excitement in the village, and although he was now in his thirties, the villagers remembered every episode of Lord Darkwood's rakish youth. Although accounted a brave solder, it was rumored that he had not changed his dissipated habits and that a feverish illness was the only thing stopping him from taking up his evil ways again.

He was, thought Annabelle bitterly, probably not a monster at all, but simply a drunken, violent brute like her husband. Mrs. Pomfret, who came in daily to do the rough cleaning, sighed over his good looks and seemed proud to have such a villain in the parish. It was amazing, reflected Annabelle, that behavior that would be deemed disgusting in a member of the lower orders was admired in an earl.

But she was in no danger of meeting him. A rich and wealthy unmarried earl would be feted by the county and would hardly stoop to visit the Carruthers. An impoverished married rake like her husband was shunned. She thought fleetingly of her husband, Guy, as he had been when they were first married. He had been merry and affectionate, and although she had never been in love with him, her life had been pleasant for a few months before he had returned to his favorite pursuits of drinking and gambling. She had learned to stay out of his way because to remonstrate with him meant a beating.

The square Norman tower of St. Charles, the church of Upper Chipping, rose above the trees. Nearly there. It had been a long walk. They could not afford a carriage. Her husband had two fine hunters, but Annabelle had never learned to ride.

She walked down the twisting, narrow village

street. The houses built of Cotswold stone gleamed a mellow gold in the sunlight. She pushed open the door of the mercers, ducking her head as she did so because she was tall and the little shop had a low-beamed ceiling. She blinked a little in the darkness of the shop. An elegant lady was being served while a tall man stood waiting beside her. Annabelle hesitated inside the doorway. The lady was finely gowned and Annabelle was now as timid of her peers as any servant girl. She knew one of her gloves had a split in one of the fingers and that the hem of her woolen gown was frayed. The lady was buying print cotton for her housemaids' dresses and the mercer was saying, "Yes, my lady. Oh, most certainly, my lady."

Who could she be? Then Annabelle with quickening curiosity remembered that wicked Lord Darkwood had a sister, a married sister at present in residence with him. What was her name? Ah, Lady Trompington. She haggled over the cost of the cotton until the price was reduced to a low enough figure. Then she demanded if there was anything new in silk.

Annabelle gave a little sigh. The ribbons would have to wait for another day. But the man with Lady Trompington heard that sigh and turned around sharply.

Annabelle stood transfixed. This must surely be Lord Darkwood. But he did not look ill in the least, or, for that matter, dissipated. Also, she was so accustomed to hearing any man with a sizable fortune described as handsome that she had expected Lord Darkwood to be nothing out of the common way.

But the tall man looking at her was simply the most handsome man she had ever seen. He had jet black hair and eyes as green as a cat, a strong nose and a thin, well-shaped mouth. His face was tanned and his figure strong. But it was the force of his personality that struck Annabelle like a blow, a heady mixture of sensuality, virility, and humor.

"Why do you not attend to this lady," said Lord Darkwood, "while my sister examines your silks at her leisure?"

Lady Trompington turned around, a smile on her face that quickly faded as her ice-cold eyes raked up and down Annabelle's shabby gown.

"Certainly, my lord," said the mercer. "What can I show you, Mrs. Carruthers?"

Feeling as gauche as a schoolgirl, Annabelle approached the counter. "I wondered if you had any silk ribbons—green, I think."

The mercer pulled out drawers and extracted spools of ribbons while Annabelle, aware of Lord Darkwood's eyes on her, felt her hands beginning to tremble. But she saw exactly what she was looking for, a pale green corded-silk ribbon that would do to embellish one of her gowns that was of light green muslin and had a nasty burn near the hem—thanks to her husband having dropped a lighted cigar on it.

She could decorate the hem and the waist with the ribbon and, with any luck, she might have enough left over for shoulder knots.

"I will take three yards," she said grandly, childishly hoping that the aristocratic customers would be impressed.

The mercer's next words hit her like a blow in the face.

"That will be six shillings, ma'am," he said, measuring out the yards and then raising his scissors.

Annabelle had only four shillings in her purse. Lord Darkwood noticed the way Annabelle's face went red and then white. With a pathetic dignity, she said, "Send the bill to the Manor, Mr. Simms."

The mercer put down his scissors with an angry little click. "You have an outstanding bill with me for four pounds, ten shillings, and twopence farthing," he said.

Annabelle was about to protest, to say that her husband had assured her he had paid that bill, but then realized in the same moment that Guy had been lying as usual.

"I am sorry, Mr. Simms," she said. "You will be paid."

The mercer gave her a cold look and then turned eagerly back to Lady Trompington.

Annabelle walked out into the sunlight. Despite the warmth of the day, she found she was shivering. And yet, why should she mind so much? The days of her marriage had been punctuated by humiliations of one sort or another and all brought about by her feckless, drunken husband's improvidence. She should have stood her ground and paid four shillings toward the outstanding bill. She half turned to go back into the shop but her courage failed her.

People were walking up and down the twisting little main street of the village, which lay in the shadow of the church tower. How happy and carefree they all seemed, thought Annabelle. Upper Chipping had two silk mills and was relatively prosperous by English village standards. It was a closed community, however, and the Carruthers had bought the Manor House a bare two years before, which marked them as outsiders.

Annabelle moved on down the street and then nearly collided with the vicar's daughter, Cressida Knight. She had been too absorbed in her own misery to see the girl and Cressida, as usual, was wrapped up tightly in one of her rosy fantasies. Cressida was a thin, intense, academic-looking sort of girl. People shook their heads over her, saying that this is what became of giving girls an education and blamed Cressida's scholarly father for the girl's rather plain looks and abstracted air, not knowing that inside Cressida's sober exterior rioted one lurid romance after another. She brightened when she saw Annabelle. Cressida thought it must be marvelous to have a handsome ruin of a husband. She often dreamt that Annabelle, whom she had previously admired from afar, would reform her husband. That was what they did in books, after all.

"Good day, Miss Knight," said Annabelle. "How d'you do?"

"I am *very* well," said Cressida. "How d'you do, Mrs. Carruthers?"

"Very well, thank you," said Annabelle, wondering what on earth Cressida would do if she replied to that polite English form of greeting that never demands a truthful answer, I am wretched. I feel alone. I am tired of being humiliated. I wish my husband would die.

Annabelle smiled and was just about to move on when the mercer came running up, rather breathless. He handed her a small package. "Lord Darkwood's compliments, Mrs. Carruthers," he said. "His lordship has settled your bill and begs you to accept these silks with his compliments."

As Annabelle's face flamed scarlet with mortification, Cressida stayed rooted to the ground. Lord

Darkwood! The wicked lord. And the attractive Mrs. Carruthers. Here was intrigue!

"Pray return the silks to his lordship with *my* compliments," said Annabelle stiffly, "and tell Lord Darkwood that Mrs. Carruthers does not accept charity and that I shall settle your bill as soon as possible."

The mercer's face hardened. "I shall return the silks, and should you choose to settle your bill, then I shall return the money to Lord Darkwood, but only then."

He turned on his heel and stuffing the package of ribbons into one capacious pocket, he strode off.

"Civil of his lordship, but very clumsy," said Cressida calmly. Cressida always sounded very practical and sensible when she spoke, having learned to keep her mad flights of fancy to herself. "You have had a sore embarrassment, Mrs. Carruthers. I was just about to return to the vicarage for tea. I beg you to join me."

"I fear I should return home," said Annabelle in a stiff voice.

"But I crave your company," said Cressida. "And Papa would be delighted to see you. Good heavens! Look at the time. Our housekeeper will be wondering where I am." Somehow without touching Annabelle, she managed to urge her along toward the vicarage.

The vicarage was a fifteenth-century building that had the appearance of having subsided comfortably into the surrounding countryside. Ivy rioted over the walls and hung about the little casement windows. Inside it was cool and dark; the parlor into which Cressida ushered Annabelle had low dark beams and a floor polished like glass.

There were bowls of spring flowers everywhere. The windows were open with gay-colored chintz curtains fluttering in the breeze.

Cressida's mother was dead. The vicarage housekeeper, a large roly-poly woman called Mrs. Jenks, promptly appeared with a laden tray. There was no sign of the vicar.

It dawned on Annabelle that she was very hungry indeed. She made light social conversation as she ate and then as she began to feel better, she studied her young hostess.

Cressida was wearing an expensive taffeta gown, but obviously one made by the local dressmaker because it was too fussy and did not flatter her thin figure. Her face was long and pale, her eyes were pale blue, and her mouth a startling red, almost as if it had been painted. She had removed her bonnet, revealing a head of fine light brown hair, which was coming out of its curl.

"Perhaps Lord Darkwood is reformed," said Cressida, finally returning to the subject that intrigued her most. "After all, all the wild stories about him concern his youth."

"And what makes you think him reformed?" asked Annabelle.

"His gift of the silks, you see. He has taken an interest in the welfare of others since his return from the wars. Old Mrs. Haggerty had been existing this age on what little food and money Papa sent her, but on his last visit, she said, she had received a visit from his lordship, who came with his man of business and arranged a monthly allowance for her; and not only for Mrs. Haggerty but for other poor widows."

"I am hardly a poor widow," said Annabelle

wryly, "and I still find his gesture vastly insulting."

"Of course you do," said Cressida calmly. "But he probably did not know who you were."

"I should think I was discussed when I left the shop," said Annabelle. "His sister, Lady Trompington, was with him and I am sure she asked a great deal of questions. She looked like that kind of lady."

"I have not met her," said Cressida, "although I have seen her in church. Very cold and proud. But you shall see her at the ball."

"Which ball?"

"Oh." Cressida colored faintly. "The earl is giving a ball and most people have been invited. Would you like Papa to speak to him? Your invitation must have been mislaid."

"No, Miss Knight," said Annabelle firmly. "Neither I nor my husband attend social functions these days."

"What a pity." Cressida poured more tea. Annabelle must go to the ball. Cressida was persuaded that the wicked earl had fallen in love with poor Mrs. Carruthers. He would challenge Mr. Carruthers to a duel, kill Mr. Carruthers, and flee to the Continent with Annabelle. They would live happily ever after in a ruined castle on the Rhine and Annabelle would invite her, Cressida, to come and visit them, For had it not been for you, my dearest of friends, I would never have found my heart's desire.

Aloud, Cressida said, "Then you must advise me on a gown to wear. What color do you think would suit me best? Papa says I should wear white, but I do not think it becomes me."

"I should be glad to," said Annabelle, "but I do

not think I should find the courage to go to the mercers with you."

"There is no need for that," said Cressida. "I have the material here. My aunt, Lady Kitson, is very rich and sends me bolts of cloth from London. I am to go to her in the Little Season for my come-out. I shall be eighteen then."

"Eighteen," said Annabelle half to herself. "How lovely. I remember being eighteen." She spoke as if she were looking back down long years instead of back over only six of them.

Cressida jumped to her feet. "Come with me, dear Mrs. Carruthers, and let me know what you think."

She led the way out of the parlor, up an old wooden staircase, and into a small room that led off to the first landing. Bolts of silks, merinos, taffetas, chintzes, and muslins were stacked up on shelves.

Annabelle blinked. "You have more cloth than the mercer," she said. "Let me see now. What would be suitable?"

She fingered the materials and then took down a bolt of ice-blue silk and took it to the window. "This, I think," said Annabelle. "It is the color of your eyes. You need a simple style with a square neckline and puffed sleeves, but with many deep flounces at the hem. High-waisted, of course. Perhaps the puff sleeves slashed to show white silk and I could make a wreath for your hair, white and blue silk roses. Yes, I think that would do. In fact, if you would allow me, Miss Knight, I could make it for you. I am a good needlewoman."

Plots raced through Cressida's mind. Annabelle must go to the ball, but she must look like a heroine so that Lord Darkwood would fall even more in love with her and fight that duel.

"I do not know what to do with the rest of the stuff," she said with affected languor. "Perhaps you would be so good as to take a bolt of the wretched stuff off my hands."

"I could not," said Annabelle, coloring up as she remembered her recent mortification.

"If you will not take something from me, then I cannot bring myself to let you make my gown," said Cressida firmly, "and so I will have to go to Mrs. Horton in the village, who will persuade Papa that I must wear white and I will look like . . . like a dog's dinner."

Annabelle laughed and capitulated. "Very well," she said. She looked at the bolts of cloth. "There is a plain white muslin there . . ."

"Oh, no," said Cressida quickly. "You have chosen for me and so I must choose for you. This rose pink silk and some of this gold. You could make a gold slip and have a pink overdress. I can just see it."

Annabelle tried to protest, but Cressida's enthusiasm was infectious and in no time at all, she found herself seated in the vicarage trap being driven back home by Cressida.

She invited Cressida into the Manor hoping the girl would refuse, but to her dismay, Cressida accepted.

Guy Carruthers was sprawled in an armchair in the yellow saloon, a decanter of brandy at his elbow. He was not wearing a cravat, and his shirt was covered with stains of snuff and last night's wine.

He looked up as the ladies entered and said viciously, "Get out of here. Demme, I don't want a cluster of chattering Friday-faced females about me.

Shoo! Be off with you." His eyes glittered in his white face and he looked half-mad.

Cressida drew a breath of pure excitement. What a villain!

"Are you sure you have sent invitations to all the village?" asked the Earl of Darkwood.

"Yes," replied his sister, letting her embroidery frame lie in her lap. "I do not know why you must entertain peasants, Charles. I could have made up a genteel group from the local county."

"I am a stickler for tradition," said her brother with a grin. "Father always asked everyone, you know that. Besides, it will give me great pleasure to see you tread a measure with the local butcher."

"Faugh! I trust these people will know their place."

"It is not Almack's, you know. I am afraid you are going to have to dance with any gentleman who asks you. Did you invite the Carrutherses from the Manor?"

Lady Trompington picked up her embroidery again and set a neat stitch. "Of course," she said in a colorless voice.

"Good. Are you inflicting anyone on us for dinner?"

"Only Mr. Knight."

"Ah, the good vicar. He has a daughter, I believe."

"Yes, but such as we do not invite the relatives of the clergy."

"How on earth have you become so hoity-toity? I blame Trompington. May I remind you that I can damned well ask anyone I feel like asking to this barn of a place?"

"Language, Charles! This is our family home and a home to be proud of," said his sister repressively.

The earl looked about him with a jaundiced eye. The late earl had left a vast fortune because he had spent little of it on his country seat. Although from the outside it seemed a fairly modern building with its fine portico, it was merely a sort of shell of an exterior to hide the old interior, which was a mixture of Elizabethan and Jacobean. The rooms were drafty and dim and were joined together by long galleries and corridors. There were low doorways and little stairs to trip the unwary. There were old suits of armor in the hall under tattered battle flags. The kitchens were a long way away from the dining room and so the food served at the table was often only lukewarm. The longest of the galleries had been chosen as the setting for the ball. Instead of paintings, mirrors had been hung along one side of it, the old earl having once gone on a visit to Versailles had had a fleeting ambition to emulate the grandeur of the French court. The cost of the mirrors had shocked him so much that his ideas had stopped there, but the present earl had judged that the gallery once it was lit by hundreds of candles would present a suitably festive air.

At dinner that afternoon, for his sister kept country hours and had ordered dinner to be served at four, the earl interrupted the gentle vicar's usual scholarly discourse to demand, "Tell me about the Carrutherses."

He was aware, although he did not turn his head, of the sudden stiffening of his sister's body.

"Ah, yes, yes," said the vicar. "Most unfortunate. Poor lady."

"Yes, *very* poor," commented Lady Trompington acidly. "We met her in the mercers this day, and her gown was shockingly shabby, and she had not even enough small change in her reticule to pay for some paltry silks."

The butler and footmen removed the cloth and placed bowls of nuts and fruit on the polished wood of the dining table along with one of those quaint miniature silver wagons on wheels containing port, sherry, burgundy, and canary.

The earl lifted out the port decanter and threw his sister a quizzical look. She rose reluctantly to her feet. "I shall leave you gentlemen to your wine," she said and rustled out of the room, the stiff taffeta skirts of her dinner gown trailing across the polished wood of the floor.

"The Carrutherses," prompted the earl gently.

"Well, my lord, I do not care for gossip . . ."

"But you do care for the welfare of those in your parish," interrupted the earl. "So feel free to tell me why Mrs. Carruthers wears shabby gowns and cannot pay her bills."

"Quite frankly, her husband is a wastrel. He drinks and gambles and now that he no longer has funds to gamble with the gentry, he drinks and gambles with the peasants at the local fairs."

"And what has Mrs. Carruthers to say to this?"

The vicar spread his hands in a deprecating gesture. "My lord, when does any woman have a say in what her husband says or does?"

"Any children?"

"No, and a good thing, too. I called on them once and Mr. Carruthers threw the decanter at my head. But my daughter, Cressida, has just befriended Mrs. Carruthers. I gather Mrs. Carruthers was humiliated by your lordship's generous offer to pay her debt at the mercers."

"Yes, I should not have done that," said the earl, studying the wine in his glass. "But I shall see the Carrutherses at the ball and make my amends."

"If I could make so bold as to advise you," said Mr. Knight, "I would suggest you do not. Mr. Carruthers has a very fiery temper. I am sure his wife told him nothing of the incident. But you have not invited them to your ball."

"On the contrary. Lady Trompington assures me that an invitation has been sent to them."

"Perhaps it was mislaid. In any case, Mrs. Carruthers herself told Cressida she had not been invited."

The earl rang the bell and asked a footman to fetch paper and ink. He wrote quickly and then sealed the letter and gave it to the waiting footman. "Take that directly to the Manor," he ordered. He turned to the vicar and smiled. "There. I have remedied matters. The Carrutherses have been invited. There is no need to tell my sister. She has been forgetful of late and I do not like to upset her by pointing out her shortcomings."

Annabelle would have refused the invitation, but her husband was spending one of his rare evenings at home. Also, he was comparatively sober, having slept in an armchair since Cressida's visit.

"Capital!" he said, scrawling an acceptance. "There will be cards, no doubt."

"No doubt," echoed Annabelle miserably.

Chapter Two

"Is your master at home, girl?"

Having no butler, Annabelle had answered the door herself. She had only two maids apart from the daily cleaning woman to help her and she had been instructing the girls in the making of rose water in the still room. She was wearing a mobcap and an apron over her gown.

"I am Mrs. Carruthers," she said with as much hauteur as she could muster. "And you, sir?"

He took off his hat and swept her a low bow that had a look of mockery about it. "Beg pardon, ma'am. I am Temple, Mr. Jonathan Temple at your service."

He handed her a card turned down at one corner to show he had called in person.

Annabelle took it. "I shall see if my husband is available," she said. "Pray enter." She left him standing in the hall and mounted the stairs to the library, hoping that her husband was sober enough to receive this visitor and hoping at the same time that Guy did not owe this Mr. Temple any money.

She found her husband in the library. He was wrapped in a banyan and with a turban on his head, but he was drinking coffee and glaring at the newspapers as if he hated every printed word.

"There is a Mr. Temple called to see you," said Annabelle.

"Who the deuce is he? Some dun?"

"No-o. He looks like a gentleman. Very fashionably dressed, almost foppish. He has fair hair and a rather weak face."

"You'll be telling me next what he has for breakfast. Show the cully up. Might be worth some sport."

Annabelle returned to the hall and asked Mr. Temple to follow her. "On your uppers, hey?" he said, looking about him as he walked up the stairs. "Good do with a mort of blunt, this place. Downright shabby I call it."

Annabelle folded her lips in a thin line but did not deign to reply. There was a rattling of carriage wheels on the drive outside, and her heart lifted. Cressida had called to take her to the vicarage for their now daily sewing session. The gowns were coming along famously and would be ready in good time for the ball in a week's time. Annabelle bit back a sigh. When she was with Cressida, she felt young and carefree and could imagine herself single again.

She pushed open the door of the library, said, "Here is Mr. Temple," and quickly walked away before Guy could start ordering her around like a servant to bring wine and cakes.

Guy Carruthers did not rise but remained slumped in his chair. "Well, well," he remarked, studying Mr. Temple lazily. "Who are you? I don't know you, do I?"

"No," replied Mr. Temple, dropping elegantly

into a chair facing Guy. "But I hope we will become good friends."

"Indeed?"

"Yes, very good friends," said Mr. Temple silkily.

Guy surveyed his visitor's rather effeminate face and foppish dress, and his face darkened. "Hey, you ain't a backgammon player, are you?"

Mr. Temple drew a pistol from his pocket and pointed it at Guy. "Imply once more that I am of that breed who prefer amors with their own sex and I shall blow your head off," he said levelly.

"Oh, the deuce. Put that toy away," said Guy. "But what am I to think if you go on smirking and talking about being friends?"

Mr. Temple put the pistol down on the table between them. "Very well," he said. "To put it bluntly, you could still be of service to us."

"Who's us? I left the military this age."

"You once helped my friends who are anxious to see Napoleon escape to freedom. You still have friends among the high-ranking military. There are certain things you could find out for us."

"I am no traitor," said Guy hotly.

"But you once took a sum of money to help your wife's friend, Emma, Comtesse Saint Juste, be abducted, did you not? A few hints in the right quarter and you would find yourself in the Tower."

"You have no proof."

"We have powerful friends close to the throne who would be happy to supply that proof. In return for your services, you would, of course, be paid a great deal of money, a certain proportion of it to be paid in advance."

Guy bit his thumb and studied Mr. Temple warily.

"How much?"

"Five hundred pounds in advance."

Guy's eyes gleamed. He then lay back in the chair and closed his eyes while he thought quickly. He was desperately in need of money. With five hundred pounds he stood a chance of making a fortune at the card tables at the earl's ball. Besides, all he had to do was then turn this silly nincompoop over to the authorities and keep the money.

He opened his eyes. "Do you have the money with you?"

"I will have it for you in a week's time. Then you will be expected to take up residence in London. There you will receive your instructions. Does your wife know of your previous . . . er . . . perfidy?"

"What, Annabelle? No. Never tell women anything. Gabbers all. All right, my friend. You come here with the money, say, next Tuesday, but come before nightfall because I have a mind to go to Darkwood's ball.

Mr. Temple smiled. He knew Guy's reputation and knew he would probably gamble away most of it at the ball, but then he would be desperate to earn more. "I agree," he said. "I don't suppose you are going to offer me any refreshment?"

"You suppose right," said Guy. "I expect you next Tuesday."

Annabelle stitched diligently at the ice-blue silk of Cressida's ballgown. She did so hope that Mr. Temple would not start Guy gambling again. Not that Guy had ever really stopped, but they had so little money that he could only afford to throw dice at the country fairs. She glanced around the comfortable parlor of the vicarage. The weather was still sunny. There were daffodils on the shaggy lawn beyond the open windows under the elm trees; bird song, peace, and tranquility. So easy to pretend she was single again and dreaming of some handsome gentleman who would fall in love with her at the ball.

"Of what are you thinking?" asked Cressida. "You had such a faraway look."

Annabelle smiled. "I was thinking of the ball," she said, and bent her head over her sewing again.

"Lord Darkwood is very handsome, is he not?" asked Cressida.

"Yes, very handsome, but such a reputation, my dear."

"All he needs is the love of a good woman," said Cressida piously.

"Now, surely you must know that rakes never reform," sighed Annabelle.

She is thinking of that husband of hers, thought Cressida. Aloud, she said, "I wonder if Lord Darkwood will dance with you, Annabelle." The new friendship was now on first name terms.

"I see no reason why he should," said Annabelle candidly. "He has a humorous glint in his eye and will no doubt dance with a few of the lowest of the village to irritate his sister. She struck me as being very high in the instep, although I only saw her for a few moments. Where is Lord Trompington?"

"On his estates. He travels to join his wife at the ball. There is a stranger in the village staying at the Crown, a Mr. Temple."

"Yes, he called to see my husband."

"An old friend?"

"No, Guy did not seem to know him."

"How very odd," said Cressida. "What was the reason for his call?"

"I did not stay to find out."

"Most odd. A mysterious stranger. Is he handsome?"

"I thought his figure too foppish and his manner too insolent," said Annabelle. "He is not known to anyone else locally."

"All I can say is," said Lady Trompington to her brother, "that the one benefit of this ball is that I shall never have to see any of these low people again on a social footing for some time."

"I would not be too sure of that," said her brother. His voice held a tinge of malice. "Our good vicar's sister is Lady Kitson."

Lady Trompington had been arranging flowers. She paused with a daffodil in one hand, her mouth hanging foolishly open. "Why did you not tell me?"

"Didn't see what difference it could possibly have made."

"But this is dreadful. Lady Kitson. Widow. Twenty thousand a year. Oh, dear, dear. I should have asked the vicar's daughter to tea. What will he think of me?"

"You are become quite incoherent, Sis. Do not exercise yourself so much. It appears Miss Cressida Knight, the daughter you have socially snubbed, has befriended Mrs. Carruthers."

"Well, of course she would!" Lady Trompington stabbed the daffodil down into the vase. "There is no other genteel company. I shall pay her particular attention at the ball."

"And yet," murmured the earl lazily, "if you do not pay her friend any attention whatsoever, our

Christian vicar and his daughter will be most offended."

"Charles, I swear you are bamming. Should I pay this Miss Knight any attention, she will no doubt be too flattered to bother about what her dowdy friend thinks!"

The earl surveyed her with admiration. "There are times when you leave me breathless," he said.

"I know," said his sister complacently. "You always did underrate my intelligence."

But when her brother had left the room, Lady Trompington became aware of the nagging little worry that had been plaguing her for the past week. Mrs. Carruthers. She remembered how Charles had settled that mercer's bill. Also, her brother had obviously made it his business to ask around the village about Mrs. Carruthers or how else would he have found out about the friendship with Miss Knight? Perhaps, of course, the vicar had told him, but she doubted that. The vicar usually confined his conversation to scholarly matters or to raising money for the common poor of Upper Chipping.

The time had definitely come to pay a call on the vicarage. With any luck, she would find Mrs. Carruthers there. Not that Mrs. Carruthers, being a married lady, was any danger to the great name of Darkwood, but still, if Charles should become sentimental over the chit, the Carrutherses might become on calling terms and Lady Trompington's pride could not bear that. She hoped the vicar would not be at home. Mr. Knight always made her feel uncomfortable. Lady Trompington would never admit to herself that the discomfort was because the vicar made her feel pretentious.

She was lucky. The vicar was locked in his study

preparing a sermon, and Miss Knight and Mrs. Carruthers were taking tea in the parlor.

Cressida was quite intimidated by Lady Trompington. The magnificence of that lady's gown, the splendor of her bonnet from which two huge ostrich feathers curled, the haughty magnified eye that surveyed her through the quizzing glass made Cressida blush and stammer. Her timid suggestion that she fetch her father was brushed aside.

"We shall have a comfortable coze, us ladies," said Lady Trompington. "It is pleasant to relax with members of one's own sex."

With that, she sank down onto the very edge of a chair, her back ramrod straight, one gloved hand resting on the tall ivory handle of a parasol and prepared to do battle. Of course there was no danger of this Mrs. Carruthers appearing at the ball. Charles did not know that she had made sure no invitation had reached her.

Annabelle was not looking her best. Guy had been in a drunken rage all that morning. She was pale and nervous, and she was wearing another shabby gown in an outmoded style. Her hair was scraped up under a muslin cap. Lady Trompington thought Mrs. Carruthers looked like a servant girl and decided to unbend a little.

But Annabelle unwittingly sabotaged all her ladyship's good intentions of trying to unbend by saying sweetly, "So kind of Lord Darkwood to invite us to the ball."

"Indeed?" Lady Trompington's stare was awful.

"Yes," said Annabelle. "His lordship sent my husband a most charming note the other day saying our invitations had been mislaid and he begged us to come."

She looked curiously at Lady Trompington, whose skin had become mottled.

"Yes, my brother must have invited every peasant in the village. Of course, once a rake, always a rake," said Lady Trompington with a thin smile.

"Are rakes Jacobite?" asked Annabelle, sounding amused while Cressida suppressed a little gasp of surprise at Lady Trompington's insolence.

"No, my dear, but so used to roistering with coachmen and tavern wenches that they are apt to forget what is due to their name. Charles is still a sad rake. I have not known him ever to fix his interest on any female for more than a fortnight."

"How sad!" exclaimed Cressida.

"Very tiresome," said Lucky Trompington. "One always must be so careful about the company one keeps. One can . . . er . . . *catch* low manners just like the common cold." She paused for effect and then continued in a pleasanter tone. "I am acquainted with your aunt Lady Kitson, Miss Knight."

"She is most kind," said Cressida. "I am to go to her in the autumn for the Little Season."

"Very good. Very good indeed. There you will find young ladies who will be a *good* influence on your character."

"I am fortunate in having the company of Mrs. Carruthers," said Cressida, beginning to become very angry.

"Poor child," sighed Lady Trompington. "Poor, poor child."

"This is too much," said Cressida, springing up. "I am going to fetch Papa."

When she had left the room, Lady Trompington realized Annabelle was fixing her with a level stare.

"I need not worry about upsetting poor Miss Knight," said Annabelle. "As long as she is gone from the room, I take leave to tell you, you are a spiteful, overdressed, bad-tempered, insufferable woman."

"You common slut," said Lady Trompington, getting quickly to her feet. "I shall tell my brother of your insults. Do not attend our ball. I command you!"

"I was under the impression that Lord Darkwood was giving the ball and not you," said Annabelle, too angry to feel dismayed.

"He will listen to me! Yes! And the good vicar. But I shall not stay in your company one second longer. Tell Mr. Knight I shall call on him."

"Tell him yourself," said Annabelle gleefully. She was normally shy and retiring and never in her life before had she been so gloriously rude.

Lady Trompington swept out. She could hardly wait to unburden herself to Charles.

But to her fury and dismay, the earl seemed mildly amused. "Got your comeuppance at last, did you?" he teased. "If there had been more Mrs. Carrutherses in your pompous life before this, dear Sis, then you might not have become quite so tiresome. Yes, I guessed you had deliberately not sent them an invitation. I have a copy of the list of people I asked you to invite. I expect not only the Carrutherses, but everyone else on that list as well!"

Lady Trompington spent the days before the ball feverishly planning ways to humiliate Annabelle Carruthers, but could not hit on any great plan except that of cutting her in front of everyone at the ball. This was not really a very good idea, though, as she was sure her brother would make up for her behavior by paying the horrible Mrs. Carruthers particular attention.

But something that she believed to have nothing at all to do with the Carrutherses put her in a good mood before the ball.

She liked shopping in the village for trifles for she enjoyed all the low bows and deep curtsies of the village people. They behaved just as they ought. She was strolling along the village street with her maid a pace behind her and her footman carrying parcels a few steps behind her maid when she almost collided with an elegantly dressed gentleman. She gave him an awful glare and made to move on, but he stopped short and swept her a low bow. "How delightful to see you again, Lady Trompington."

Lady Trompington raised her quizzing glass and studied the man before her. He was wearing a curly-brimmed beaver on top of pomaded curls. His shirt points were so high and stiff that they dug into his cheeks. His cravat, to Lady Trompington's un-schooled eye, seemed to be a miracle of starched muslin. He was wearing a blue coat with a dog-skin collar over a biscuit-colored coat with large brass buttons. His trousers, which appeared to have been painted on his rather thin legs, were canary yellow and his Hessians shone like black glass.

"We met at my aunt's musicale last Season," murmured Mr. Temple, for it was he. "The Duchess of Norton."

A dawning smile thawed the ice of Lady Trompington's face.

"My card," said Mr. Temple, proffering one with another deep bow.

"Why, what brings you to Upper Chipping?" asked Lady Trompington.

It had not taken Mr. Temple long to find out Guy Carruthers's dreadful reputation in the village. He rightly decided it would not endear him to Lady Trompington to state he was visiting the Manor. He wanted an invitation to that ball to keep an eye on Carruthers. He had already waylaid the earl, but to little effect. Lord Darkwood had looked unimpressed by the mention of the ducal aunt. It did not dawn on Mr. Temple that it was because the earl was fairly sure the relationship was a fiction.

"I am recovering from a fever," said Mr. Temple, "and felt in need of some country air before the rigors of the Season begin."

"We are honored to have you in Upper Chipping," said Lady Trompington. "Do you reside here long?"

"Perhaps another few days." Mr. Temple looked wistful. "I pine for civilized society. The company of bumpkins does not amuse me."

"So fatiguing," agreed Lady Trompington. "I wish *I* could offer you some civilized society, Mr. . . ." She glanced at his card. "Temple. But all we have to offer is some sad romp of a ball given by my brother, Darkwood, to which he has invited every turnip head in the village."

Mr. Temple's wistful look increased. "But *you* would be there . . ."

He allowed his voice to trail away in a question.

"If you think you would not find it all sadly provincial," said Lady Trompington, "do pray attend. We would be honored to have your company."

"I would count myself honored if I could manage to have one dance with you," said Mr. Temple, raising her gloved hand and kissing the air an inch above the back of it.

Lady Trompington actually blushed. "Of course, you may have your dance," she said graciously. She then gave him instructions as to the time of the ball and how to get there, not knowing he already knew both, and took her leave, after throwing him an almost flirtatious look.

Annabelle had lost her courage. Mr. Knight told her the next day after that disastrous scene, that Lady Trompington had called on him and had said very harsh words about this Mrs. Carruthers. Although the vicar obviously thought the earl's sister a very nasty lady, indeed, Annabelle now dreaded the thought of meeting her again. Guy would probably be drunk, and she was sure Lady Trompington would make the most of that.

But all through the day of the ball, Guy showed no signs of picking up the brandy decanter. He was, however, as restless as a cat and as the sun began to set, took to pacing up and down the hall.

Annabelle, up in her bedchamber enjoying a warm bath in front of the fire, heard a carriage arrive and wondered who could possibly have come to call.

She sent one of the maids to find out and on hearing it was Mr. Temple decided to stay abovestairs until that young man had left.

Meanwhile, in the library, Guy had grabbed at the five hundred pounds that Mr. Temple had brought him. Gambling fever burned in his eyes, and he barely heard what Mr. Temple was saying.

"You have not been listening, my friend," said Mr. Temple. "Part of the arrangement is that you should leave for London on the morrow."

"Hey, what? So soon?"

"Time for you to earn your wages."

Guy's eyes narrowed. "I don't like your tone, sir-rah."

"Odso? Then hand back the money for we have means to make you work for us for naught."

"The devil you have," said Guy sulkily. "Oh, demme, sit down and have a glass of something."

"I fear I do not have the time. I must return to the inn to change for this ball."

"You've been invited?" Guy cursed inwardly. He did not want Mr. Temple hanging about the card tables like a death's head.

"Yes, Lady Trompington has taken a liking to me. Before I leave, I must remind you that you must never say anything of our dealings to your wife."

"What d'ye take me for? Wouldn't dream of it."

"Good. Till this evening."

After he had left, Guy looked longingly at the brandy decanter and then at the clock. Best to keep a clear head. Besides, he did not have a valet and must dress himself for the evening. Better get ready.

After an hour and a half, he succeeded in dressing himself to his satisfaction. The tying of his cravat had only taken half an hour. He was wearing a dark green coat and knee breeches with clocked stockings and dancing pumps. He was standing in the drawing room, admiring himself in the mirror over the fireplace, when his wife entered.

He stood very still, looking at her reflection in the mirror.

She was wearing a gold silk gown with a rose silk overdress, the hem of which was embroidered in a gold key pattern. The low neckline revealed the excellence of her breasts. Her thick and glossy hair

30

curled from under a gold and pink turban, made in the style shown in the famous portrait of Lord Byron where he is dressed as a Turk. She looked very beautiful, almost like the sweet and carefree girl he had married. He felt a thickness in his throat, and the easy tears of the habitual drunkard sprang to his eyes.

"By Jove," he said, turning around. "If you ain't a picture."

"You look very fine yourself," said Annabelle happily. She was happy because he was sober and because he looked more like the handsome man she had once known.

"We'll be the best couple there," he said, walking forward and taking her hands.

But as he walked forward and looked down into her face, for he was well over six foot tall, he saw the trace of sadness that was always there now in her eyes. A shiver ran through him and he pressed her hands tightly. "I shouldn't tell you this," he said, "but, demme, one never knows what will happen. Should I die, my dear, I've left a letter written to you. You know that little secret cupboard behind the paneling in my bedchamber? I've left it there. But don't ever look at it till after I'm dead."

"Oh, Guy, don't speak of such things. Perhaps . . . oh, perhaps if you were not to drink so much, you would not think of death or . . . or . . . gamble so much."

He dropped her hands and turned away with a scowl. "Always preaching and moralizing," he said bitterly. "I think I've married a Methodist."

"I'm sorry Guy. It's just that . . . ."

"Just nothing!" he snapped. "Get your shawl, and let's get out of here!"

Annabelle arranged a fine Norfolk shawl about her shoulders, mentally chiding herself for having made her husband angry. Surely she should have known by now the futility of trying to remonstrate with him about his drinking and gambling.

There was a full moon as they walked together down the drive, Mr. and Mrs. Carruthers, members of the gentry, who did not possess one carriage. The notes crackled in Guy's pocket when he slipped his hand inside to feel their bulk. He should have left most of it at home, but he felt lucky. He felt sure the bad days were over. After the ball, he would turn Temple over to the authorities and let him squeal his head off. Guy began to feel happy again. Friends close to the crown, indeed! And he had believed him! No, Temple was a charlatan. But, wait, why kill the goose that was laying the golden eggs? Surely Temple would pay dear for his, Guy Carruthers's silence? Guy began to laugh. Annabelle asked him nervously what it was that was amusing him so much, but he only gave her a quick hug and said he was happy because they were together. Annabelle smiled at him and took his hand in hers, relieved that his bad mood had gone.

Chapter Three

Most of the guests had already arrived by the time Annabelle and Guy made their way up the long drive that led through the Darkwood estates to the earl's home, Delaney.

Guy was always late for everything and Annabelle had become accustomed to this irritating habit of his, for to try to rush him meant he would sulk and then they would be even later.

Annabelle trudged along, the iron rings on her pattens clanking on the ground. How awful to arrive in these dreadful clog things. But the ground was still damp, and she could not risk soiling her dancing slippers.

At last they came in sight of the house. Annabelle was not yet old enough to have all hope and youth and romanticism beaten out of her. All the windows were ablaze with candlelight and there came the jaunty sound of fiddle and drum across the night air and Annabelle's heart lifted. Just for this one evening, she would forget her troubles and enjoy the ball. She was even able to face up to the likelihood of some terrible snub from Lady Trompington with equanimity. Because of her friendship with Cressida, she had come to know many of the village people. Most of them had been learning the new dance, the quadrille, in the village hall. Cressida said that Jem Hunt, the grocer's boy, had become so adept at the steps that he danced like the veriest beau.

She could sense the rising excitement in her husband, but he could not be looking forward to any gambling. They did not have any money and, in any case, she doubted if a country ball would offer any higher sport at the card tables than Pope Joan and silver loo.

They separated from each other in the hall to leave their cloaks in the respective rooms allotted to ladies and gentlemen. Annabelle was glad the dressing room for the ladies was empty except for a maid, sitting in a corner.

She carefully checked her appearance in the glass. Yes, she had done well. There was nothing in her dressmaking to show that she had made it herself. It was as good as anything that might have come from the hands of a London couturiere.

She went back into the hall and joined Guy, and together they mounted the long stairs to the gallery where the ball was being held. Because they were late, the earl, his sister, and her husband had left their position at the top of the stairs to join their guests in the ballroom.

Sets were dancing the quadrille with that intense worried look on their faces that quadrille dancers have as they try to remember the intricate steps. The earl came forward to greet them, his eyebrows lifting slightly as he recognized Annabelle. A smile curved his mouth. He knew his sister's nose would be put out of joint by the style and elegance of Mrs. Carruthers's gown. Her eyes were very beautiful he noticed, an odd sort of deep gray, fringed with thick lashes.

He began to talk easily to Guy about crops and horses. Lady Trompington came up to join them, her eyes snapping. "You are neglecting your other guests, Charles."

"I shall get to them presently," he said mildly. "Mrs. Carruthers you have already met. May I present her husband, Mr. Guy Carruthers."

Lady Trompington held out two fingers for Guy to shake. He stared at them, his color rising, and then gave a little shrug and seized her whole hand and shook it vigorously. Annabelle meanwhile had been aware that Jem Hunt, the grocer's boy, was being urged by his friends to ask Lady Trompington to partner him in the next quadrille. To Annabelle's dismay, Jem approached them. She had a wild hope that Jem might ask her and so avoid a dreadful snub, but Jem bowed gracefully before Lady Trompington and said, "Pray do me the very great honor, my lady, of allowing me to partner you in the next quadrille."

There was an awful silence.

Now Jem did not look like a country bumpkin. He looked more like a sort of village Adonis. Although his clothes were coarse, he was tall, slim, and had golden hair, wide blue eyes, and a Greek profile.

"Know your place, my good man," said Lady Trompington frostily, "and solicit some village maiden instead."

Annabelle stepped forward. "And here is one lady who would consider it a very great honor to dance with you, Mr. Hunt."

Jem looked at her in a dazed way as she gently

tugged at his sleeve and guided him to the floor. She thought she heard the earl say, "Bravo."

"I'm mort ashamed," whispered Jem. "I should never have had the impertinence to ask her. Reckon her'll probably get her husband to horsewhip me."

"Nonsense," said Annabelle lightly as they stood together in the set. "Where is Lord Trompington?"

"Little gentleman over there," said Jem, giving a discreet nod.

Annabelle looked across the room to where a little man with a face like a tortoise stood. He was painted, rouged, pomaded, and corseted and with his round shoulders, large belly, and thin shanks managed to look remarkably like Mr. Punch.

"I don't think he's up to horsewhipping you," said Annabelle with an infectious giggle.

Jem began to laugh as well, and then he saw his friends were regarding him with awed admiration and laughed the more.

The quadrille began. Jem was an exquisite dancer. Annabelle was graceful and knew the steps well.

Lady Trompington stood and watched them, seething with fury. Her brother had told her in no uncertain terms that since she had refused to dance with Jem Hunt, then she could not dance with any other gentleman. But worse was to come. She had been triumphant at managing to persuade Lady Clairmont to attend, having learned that the star of London society was visiting friends in the neighborhood. Lady Clairmont was a leader of the ton. Everyone copied her clothes and her manners and even the stern patronesses of Almack's were said to be in awe of her.

She was a dark-haired woman with a rather severe face and a high-bridged nose. She was accounted a great beauty because she was very rich and dressed in the latest fashions.

She approached Lady Trompington, and said, "I insist you introduce me to that Greek god who is dancing with that pretty woman in the French gown."

"I doubt if it is French," said Lady Trompington. "She is a Mrs. Carruthers, and the Carrutherses do not have a feather to fly with."

"You fascinate me. I will have an introduction to her first and find out where she got that gown. There is another exquisite gown here being worn by the vicar's daughter of all people. In any case, who is that divine young man?"

"He is the grocer's boy, so naturally you will no longer be interested in meeting him," said Lady Trompington.

"Oh, but I am," said Lady Clairmont with a brittle laugh. "Beauty is classless, and it is only very common people who despise others for their low birth or lack of money. Ah, here is Darkwood. I crave an introduction to that handsome couple, Mrs. Carruthers and her country swain."

"And you shall have it," said the earl. "Beautiful, are they not?"

Lady Trompington turned and walked away. To her relief, she was approached by Mr. Temple, who treated her to all the courtesy and deference she considered due to her.

"I have been hoping that you have a dance to spare me," said Mr. Temple.

Not for worlds would Lady Trompington admit her brother had forbidden her to dance. She would need to explain the reason why and the countess's remarks still rankled.

"I am afraid I have the headache," she said. The quadrille had finished and a waltz was being announced. Her brother was introducing Mrs. Carruthers and Jem Hunt to Lady Clairmont. Then Jem was leading Lady Clairmont to the floor and the earl was partnering Mrs. Carruthers.

"Where is Mr. Carruthers?" asked Mr. Temple.

"In the card room, I believe," said Lady Trompington.

"He cannot do much damage to what is left of the Carrutherses' money by playing ladies' games," commented Mr. Temple.

"The stakes may be high, alas," said Lady Trompington. "My brother has invited some old army friends, and I know that three of them at least are hardened gamblers."

Mr. Temple's small mouth curved in a smile. A hungry Guy Carruthers would be a Guy Carruthers ready to serve the French cause. "Do you know Carruthers?" he became aware Lady Trompington was asking him.

"Slightly," he said. "Only slightly." He had already noticed with amusement that Lady Trompington was jealous of the stylish and attractive Mrs. Carruthers. "Mrs. Carruthers and Darkwood make a splendid couple," he went on with a tinge of malice in his voice.

Lady Trompington raised her quizzing glass. The earl and Annabelle were circling gracefully to the strains of the waltz. In the gallery's many mirrors, their multiple reflections seemed to taunt her. He was smiling down at Annabelle Carruthers in a way that no gentleman should smile when partnering a married woman. There was a certain fleeting tenderness in his eyes that alarmed his sister.

As the waltz came to an end and the couples bowed and curtsied, Lady Trompington, with a feeling of relief, saw Lady Clairmont's daughter, Rosamund, entering the room on the arm of her father, Sir Edward. The earl had never met Rosamund before, and his sister was sure that to see Rosamund was to love her and that the threat of Annabelle Carruthers would fade away like the mist on the ornamental lake at Delaney in bright sunlight. She was not worried that her brother would start an affair with Mrs. Carruthers, but only that the Carrutherses might become on visiting terms with the earl.

Rosamund Clairmont *was* beautiful. She had glossy black hair with a natural curl, pure white skin, and very red lips. Her figure was exquisite and shown to advantage in a gown of near-transparent muslin worn over a diaphanous pink underdress. Her eyes were her most arresting feature. They were of a brilliant blue, almond-shaped, giving all the innocence of eighteen years the allure of a temptress. She knew how to use them to advantage, too, her glance sliding and teasing. Lady Clairmont welcomed her daughter and husband and introduced them to the earl and Annabelle.

Sir Edward was a tall, handsome man with the same arresting eyes as the daughter on his arm on whom he obviously doted. Lady Trompington hurried up to join them after throwing Mr. Temple a brief smile of farewell over one bony shoulder. She ignored Annabelle completely and focused her whole attention on Rosamund. "Darling girl," she cooed. "You look more beautiful than ever. Do you not think so, brother?"

"Miss Clairmont is charming," said the earl, "but I have no previous occasion with which to compare her beauty, this being the first time I have met her. But I sincerely hope, not the last." He raised Rosamund's hand to his lips. Annabelle stood a little to one side, feeling rejected, forgotten.

Rosamund smiled up at the earl with a teasing, mocking expression in her eyes. "I hope this will prove to be the first of many meetings, my lord," she said, "so that you may soon be able to have comparisons and tell me I have sadly gone off in looks."

The earl laughed, and Annabelle thought crossly, Why does he laugh? She did not say anything funny.

"And such an exquisite gown!" exclaimed Lady Trompington. "You must have had it made in London."

"Yes," said Rosamund. "Mama had it fashioned for me when we were last in town. I felt quite soigné until I met Mrs. Carruthers."

Lady Trompington gave a shrill laugh, her eyes encouraging Lady Clairmont to share the joke, but Lady Clairmont had already noticed an acquaintance on the other side of the gallery and she merely bowed and moved away on the arm of her husband. "My dearest child," said Lady Trompington, "you are too kind, but how can you compare the work of a village dressmaker with that of a London couturiere?"

Annabelle stiffened angrily, and Rosamund, seeing the quick flash of irritation in the earl's eyes, said with a rippling laugh, that laugh young girls were trained to make by their music masters, starting on a high note and running down the scale, "Come now, Lady Trompington, such exquisite and graceful work is too masterly to have been fashioned in the country. Pray tell us the name of your dressmaker, Mrs. Carruthers."

"I designed and made it myself," said Annabelle.

"La! What a paragon! Come, promenade with me for a little, Mrs. Carruthers, and I shall try to divine the secrets of your art." She smiled up into the earl's eyes before linking her arm in Annabelle's and leading her away.

But Rosamund did not want to talk about gowns. She had seen the earl with Mrs. Carruthers and how he had looked at her. She wanted to find out whether Annabelle was married or not, whether the earl's attentions were seriously engaged elsewhere, and whether he had a mistress tucked away somewhere.

They walked together along the gallery, their reflections walking with them along the long row of mirrors. There was a break in the dancing and people were sitting in red velvet-covered benches along the wall or standing in little groups, conversing.

"You must tell me all you know about Darkwood," said Rosamund, her grip on Annabelle's arm surprisingly strong.

"I do not know him at all, really," said Annabelle. "In fact, I have not spoken to him before this evening."

She blushed and Rosamund studied her curiously. Annabelle was blushing because she was remembering the intensity of her physical emotions when she had danced with the earl, of how she had meant to reproach him over the matter of the silks and the mercer's bill, but his sheer proximity had all but taken her breath away.

"He is very handsome, is he not?" pursued Rosamund. She was wearing a very heavy perfume and that, combined with the heat from all the candles burning brightly in candelabra in the gallery, was making Annabelle feel quite ill. They walked out of the gallery and stood together on a wide circular landing. The card room was opposite and the door stood open. Guy was playing cards, his face flushed and his eyes glittering. As Annabelle watched, Mr. Temple approached and said something to Guy and laid a hand on his arm, but Guy merely scowled and brushed him off.

"I said, he is very handsome," repeated Rosamund.

"Darkwood? Oh, yes, very," said Annabelle.

"Is your husband here?"

"Yes, he is in the card room."

Rosamund gave a pleased smile. So pretty Mrs. Carruthers was not a widow. One obstacle out of the way.

"Is Darkwood engaged or otherwise spoken for?"

"I do not believe so, but then, Miss Clairmont, as I have already said, I know little about him. Your mother would be better informed than I."

Rosamund pouted, a mocking pout. "But how can I ask Mama indiscreet questions? The reason I am asking *you*, Mrs. Carruthers, is because you are so mundane and so much younger than Mama. I am persuaded you cannot be stuffy."

Despite her desire to get away from Rosamund's rather cloying personality, Annabelle laughed. "Oh, I can be surprisingly stuffy, even if I do make my own gowns."

Rosamund tapped her playfully on the arm with her fan. "Stoopid! Tell me, have you heard the whispers that the earl has a mistress?"

"I do not hear whispers about anything, Miss Clairmont. This occasion is unusual. I do not go about in society."

Rosamund looked restlessly about, seeming to have lost interest in Annabelle. "Well," she said languidly, "I overheard some London ladies saying he had an opera dancer in town."

Annabelle felt suddenly depressed. While she had been dancing with the earl, she had imagined herself carefree and young. For some reason, Rosamund's remark brought her down to earth with a bump. She had felt for a little while that the earl held her in special regard, and that had done wonders for her spirits. But he was merely an accomplished flirt and she was the impoverished Mrs. Carruthers, married to a drunk and a wastrel, and had spent a precious part of the evening allowing herself to be questioned about the amors of a rake by a silly girl. All at once she longed for Matilda, Duchess of Hadshire, with her forthright, bracing manner.

"If you want to know more about the earl," she said, "then you must ask someone else. Oh, here is Miss Knight." With relief, Annabelle watched Cressida approaching them and privately thought that the vicar's daughter had never looked better. A little rouge gave her normally pale face some much needed color, and the gown flattered her figure.

"I am in alt," sighed Cressida, after the introductions were made. "So many compliments on my gown. The dancing is about to commence again."

Rosamund gave a stifled little exclamation. If the earl were ever to have a chance to ask her to dance, then she must be in the ballroom, ready and waiting. But she was too late. The earl was already leading some "dowdy village female"—as Rosamund damned her—onto the floor. She saw one of the village boys approaching her and treated him to a look of frozen hauteur so that he veered away from her with his eyes averted as if he had been meaning to ask someone else.

Mr. Temple was becoming increasingly worried. Guy was admittedly playing deep, but he was winning steadily. He wondered whether he should try to find some way to put a stop to the gambling. On the other hand, surely it was better to let Guy play on than risk his leaving the table with money. His luck could surely not last much longer. He saw Lady Trompington smiling at him and made his way quickly to her side. He considered her worth cultivating. She might be able to pick up some military gossip for him if he handled her deftly enough. He made his way quickly to her side and begged to be allowed to escort her to the supper room. Lady Trompington, who had been about to go into supper with her husband, promptly agreed. Lord Trompington looked after his departing wife in a startled way before going off to find another partner.

The earl was approaching Annabelle when he saw her being claimed by her husband and so offered his arm to Rosamund instead. He thought her a pretty little thing with engaging ways.

Annabelle was delighted to discover that Guy was sober. Not only that, but he whispered to her that he had just won over one thousand pounds.

"Why do you not give it to me for safekeeping," urged Annabelle, "and play no more this evening."

But Guy looked at her mulishly and said he had only just begun to make their fortune. "I saw two magpies in the woods this afternoon," he said. "A sure sign my luck has turned."

"Then keep a clear head," begged Annabelle. "How did you come by the money to gamble for such high stakes?"

The sober Guy felt a sharp pang of guilt and was all at once determined to drown it. He held out his glass to a footman for wine. He drained it in one gulp and held up his glass for more and growled, "Mind your own business."

Annabelle thought dismally that it would have been better had she held her tongue. Guy now seemed determined to celebrate his winnings. She looked across the room to where the earl sat with Rosamund. His jet black hair gleamed like a blackbird's wing in the candlelight, and his hooded eyes shone green like emeralds. The face was strong and sensual, and yet the mouth was thin and hard. What would it be like to be kissed by that mouth? The earl seemed to be highly entertained by whatever Rosamund was saying but then, as if conscious of Annabelle's gaze, he looked across directly at her, his green eyes glinting, and she quickly looked away.

Her heart was pounding. There had been something disturbingly predatory and almost possessive about the earl's gaze. She glanced back at him under her lashes. He was smiling down at Rosamund.

Annabelle felt very low and flat, all her enjoyment of the ball, which had briefly come back, melting away, leaving her on a desolate shore full of jagged rocks marked *debt* and *loneliness*. It was strange to be a married lady and yet feel so alone. All she wanted to do was to go home and get into bed and hide under the bedclothes. Rosamund, for example, had all the world at her pretty feet. She was young and beautiful and rich. She would not have to rise early on the morrow to help the maids clean a drafty and decaying house and wonder if the butcher would possibly allow any more credit. One thousand pounds! If only Guy would give her a little of that money. Plucking up her courage, she turned to her husband.

"Guy," she whispered, "we have so many outstanding bills in the village that only a fraction of your winnings would settle. Please let me have just a little . . . in case you lose it all."

He glared at her for a moment, and then his face softened. She was looking so elegant and so pretty. Demme. There wasn't a female in the room to touch her. He fished in his pocket and pulled out a handful of notes.

"There you are, puss," he said indulgently. "Pay your tradesmen."

"Thank you," whispered Annabelle, stuffing the notes in her reticule. Now if only by some miracle the card playing could be canceled for the rest of the evening.

Mr. Temple was thinking pretty much the same thing. If Guy continued to win . . . Of course, he was drinking heavily.

He looked across the room. Guy Carruthers was drinking deep. His face was flushed, and there was a slackness about his mouth. So Mr. Temple, who had been about to persuade Lady Trompington to close the card room, decided to remain silent. He did not know that apart from being able to invite a few guests of her own to the ball, Lady Trompington had little control over anything in her brother's house.

Supper was at last over and most of the guests went back to the ballroom while Guy and his gambling companions returned to the tables. The earl knew the stakes were high but in an age when men lost as much as twenty-five thousand pounds in a night at one of the clubs in St. James's, he barely thought about the amount of money that was changing hands at his ball.

Annabelle began to worry more and more. She was now convinced that Guy would lose the money, and then he would come in search of her and take away the money he had given her. All the tradesmen they owed money to were at the ball, for it was a typical country ball, although Lady Trompington might sneer and say it was as bad as the servants' Christmas dance. But she could hardly go around paying them off in front of everyone.

Jem Hunt, the grocer's boy, approached her and begged another dance. Annabelle thought quickly. She drew him aside.

"Jem, you know how things stand with us," she said urgently. "We owe most of the tradesmen in the village money. I wish to pay them off now, but I do not know how to do it. My husband gave me some money, and if I do not pay the bills, I fear I shall lose it before the evening is out."

Jem looked at her sympathetically. Guy Carruthers's gambling was well-known in the village. He knew the beautiful Mrs. Carruthers meant that if she did not get rid of the money quickly, then her husband would emerge from the card room and take it from her.

"If you will trust me with it, ma'am," he said eagerly, "I could pay them off discreetly and return the rest of the money to you."

"Oh, would you, Jem? Step outside to the landing with me, and I will give you what I have in my reticule."

The earl watched them go, wondering what was happening. He strolled over to the doorway of the long gallery and looked out. Mrs. Carruthers was giving the local Adonis a sheaf of notes.

He leaned against the wall and watched. He saw Annabelle return, an expression of relief on her face. The vicar's daughter came up to her and both walked off together. Then Jem entered the room looking self-conscious and important. The earl raised his quizzing glass. He saw Jem approach his master, the grocer, and whisper in his ear. Notes changed hands. Then he went on to the butcher and the same thing happened, and then the mercer.

So Mrs. Carruthers is paying her tradesmens' bills, thought the earl. She does not have much faith in her husband's luck this evening.

He went along to the card room. Guy Carruthers appeared wild and disheveled. He was wearing his coat inside out for luck. The earl studied the play. It did not take him long to realize that Guy was losing heavily.

Then Guy said, "I shall be back in a trice." The earl followed him out. Annabelle was dancing a country reel with the vicar. The earl could see Guy waiting impatiently for the dance to finish. Then he approached his wife. The earl saw Annabelle shake her head and saw Guy's face darken with anger. He took a half step forward for he was afraid Guy was about to strike his wife. Then Guy turned on his heel and went back to the card room. The earl saw him later propped against the wall, no longer part of the game, watching the play with hungry eyes.

Mr. Temple, too, had been watching Guy. He was delighted with Guy's losses, for Guy had not only lost his winnings, but had gambled away the Manor as well.

He'll be ready for work now, thought Mr. Temple with satisfaction.

Guy saw him standing at the entrance to the card room and hope lit in his eyes.

He crossed the room and joined Mr. Temple. "Where can we talk?" he asked.

"There's bound to be a room somewhere," said Mr. Temple. "Follow me, dear friend."

He pushed open a door next to the card room. It was a small morning room with delicate furniture and gold and white striped paper on the walls.

"I need more money . . . now," said Guy.

"You will get more as soon as you start work for us in London," said Mr. Temple, looking amused.

Guy smiled slowly. "No, my dear friend, I think you will pay up and pay up gladly when you find out what I have to say. If you do not pay me, then I shall go to the authorities and denounce you as a traitor."

Mr. Temple's face darkened. "You would not dare. You would damn yourself. You have already accepted money from us."

"And where's your proof?" jeered Guy. "Stupid of you, wasn't it? You didn't even ask for a receipt. I don't believe a word of all this rot of having powerful friends. What can you do? Take me to court? Stand up there and damn yourself as a traitor in order to convict me? So pay now."

Mr. Temple took a snuffbox from his pocket and helped himself to a pinch of snuff with maddening slowness. His foppish face betrayed nothing, but he was thinking furiously. Things had not worked out the way his superiors had planned. They had said Guy had worked easily for them before. He was a shiftless wastrel who could be used and then discarded. But Guy Carruthers must be silenced for the moment until he could think what to do.

"I am not a walking bank," he said at last. "I have a hundred pounds on me, nothing more."

"That'll do," said Guy feverishly. "I'll take that now, and you call on me tomorrow and be prepared to pay for my silence."

"As you will," said Mr. Temple calmly. He pulled a wad of notes out of his pocket. Guy grabbed them and rushed from the room.

But when he returned to the card room, it was to find it closed and locked. The earl had learned that Guy had lost the Manor and had persuaded his friends to stop the play. He wondered what on earth to do. He wanted to help Mrs. Carruthers, but that was a job for her husband. His friend, Captain Jamieson, had won the Manor from Guy. To suggest to the captain that he tear up the IOU was unthinkable. Gambling debts were debts of honor. Well, Mrs. Carruthers had chosen to marry a gambler, thought the earl, forgetting that women usually had little say in whom they married.

He felt bored, restless and tired playing lord of the manor in this sleepy corner of the Cotswolds. The past ten years had been spent in one battle in the Peninsula after another, ending on the field of Waterloo. He might tell himself he was tired of death and carnage, but the risk and excitement of battle had not left him.

Perhaps what he needed was a wife. It would be fun to have sons and teach them to hunt and shoot. His eye fell on Rosamund, who smiled at him, and he felt his pulses quicken. That glinting sideways glance of hers promised so much.

But as the next waltz was announced, he somehow found himself bowing before Annabelle. Soon his hand was at her waist and he was circling the floor with her, conscious of her nearness, of the pliancy of her body, of the sweet flower perfume she wore. There was something so vulnerable and feminine about her, a woman to cherish and protect.

"Have you enjoyed yourself?" he asked.

Annabelle looked into his eyes and said, "Yes, my lord. Thank you for inviting us." But there was a world of sadness there. He thought he would like to see her laugh. She was too young to be so worried and sad.

Rosamund, dancing with Captain Jamieson, tried to listen to what he was saying while keeping her eyes on the earl. Her mother had told her that the earl planned to open his town house. In London she would have the field to herself with no disturbingly attractive Mrs. Carruthers around to take the earl's attention away. Rosamund was not worried about the earl's rumored mistress. All gentlemen had at least one in keeping. Ladies turned a blind eye to such things. Rosamund knew the earl to be the biggest available catch on the marriage market and it was ambition rather than desire that fueled her determination to get him.

The earl had no sooner finished dancing with Annabelle than Guy lumbered up, drunk and angry.

"Come along," he said sharply to his wife. "Time to go home. The evening's gone curst flat."

Annabelle swept a low curtsy to the earl and quietly took her husband's arm, trying to steady him as Guy staggered from the long gallery. The earl watched the pair for a moment and then with a little shrug went in search of Rosamund.

Chapter Four

GUY STAGGERED AND REELED down the drive. Annabelle had released his arm when they were clear of the house, and she walked behind him, the iron rings on the soles of her pattens striking sparks from the frosty pebbles on the drive. Trees with their tiny new leaves stood out black against the starry sky like fine lace. Some water bird hooted mournfully from the lake echoing the desolation in Annabelle's heart.

She knew about Guy gambling away the Manor because he had told her, just outside the house, defiantly and drunkenly, almost proudly, as if the loss of their country home had elevated him to the top league of gamblers. They still had the town house, he had said, and they would travel there as soon as possible. Jamieson was welcome to that ruin of a place.

Now all Annabelle wanted to do was get to bed. She blessed that custom of the upper classes of having separate bedrooms. Guy hardly ever visited her bedroom, and when he did, it was a distressingly drunken fumble rather than lovemaking.

She let him get well ahead of her. Carriages of the departing guests passed them on the drive, their faces momentarily lit by the carriage lamps inside, driving past secure in a rich world, not one looking out at the figures trudging down the long drive.

By the time they turned in at the gates of the Manor, Annabelle was shivering with cold. There would be no fires in the bedrooms. The woodpile had dwindled away, and there were no outdoor menservants to cut more.

Guy, ahead of her, let himself into the large square house and left the door open behind him. He did not even turn around to see if she were there.

Annabelle went into the blackness of the hall and groped on the side table for a candle. Guy had already lit his and was mounting the stairs, a small circle of wavering candlelight showing his uneven passage.

She picked up her own candle and followed slowly up the stairs and turned in at her own bedroom door.

Sanctuary! For one night. She carefully took off her beautiful dress and hung it away in the wardrobe, hoping she would have a chance to wear it again in London. She shivered as she washed her face and hands in cold water and then, quickly stripping off her underclothes, she pulled a nightgown over her head and climbed into bed.

Sleep came quickly, blessed sleep. But almost immediately she began to dream. She was dancing the waltz on the lawns in front of Delaney with the earl. The day was sunny and warm. He held her closer and closer and then he tilted her chin up and his lips approached hers. But she twisted her mouth away. He was smoking a cheroot and the smoke from it, burning in his left hand, was strong and acrid. She choked and flapped at the smoke, and he began to laugh.

Annabelle awoke. The smoke was not in her dream but all about her. There was a red light under her door. She darted from her bed and opened it and then quickly slammed it shut again in the face of the red and crackling inferno of fire that lay outside. She ran to the window and opened it. The two maids were on the lawn in their nightclothes, screaming loudly and pointing upward. Annabelle seized a cloak and pulled it on over her nightgown. She thrust her feet into a pair of slippers and then began to climb out of the window, grasping tight hold of the ivy outside. She swung herself out and hung motionless for a moment and then scrabbled with her feet until she found a hold in the ivy. Slowly, she began to descend, her ears full of the roaring and crackling of the fire. She heard shouts from the driveway now and the galloping of horses' hooves. Inch by inch, she felt her way down, trying not to panic. She did not think of Guy's safety, instinctively feeling Guy would be all right. God protected drunks and little children. Strong arms grasped her and lifted her to the ground, and she heard the earl's voice say sharply, "Who else is in the house?"

"Only my husband," said Annabelle, twisting around and looking at him, her eyes dilated. "But he must have escaped."

The earl caught her up in his arms, strode off with her, and then put her down on the grass next to the two maids who were still sobbing and crying. The village fire engine was sending a jet of water into the flames, a thin weak jet that seemed mocked by the raging inferno of the building.

Soon the lawn in front of the house was full of people. Men had formed a chain from a weedy pond to the house and were passing along buckets of water. There was no sign of Guy.

Cressida and her father, the vicar, drove up. "Come away, Annabelle," said Cressida. "You cannot stand here in the cold."

"My husband," said Annabelle through white lips. "What has happened to Guy?"

And then by the light of the still raging flames, she saw the earl and his friends carrying a body clear of the house.

Shaking off Cressida's restraining hand, Annabelle ran forward.

"He tried to escape," said the earl gently, "but broke his neck in the fall."

Annabelle sank to her knees beside the body of her husband. He must have gone to sleep in his clothes, she thought, bewildered. He reeked of brandy. The smell was appalling. He smelled as if he had been doused in brandy.

She became aware of Cressida's arms around her and Cressida's voice in her ear. "Come away. You cannot do anything here."

"Yes, go," said the earl harshly.

Numbly she allowed herself to be led away. She sat huddled in a corner of the vicarage trap, moving away from the red light of the fire, unable to believe that Guy was dead. Surely he would spring up and laugh drunkenly and say he had done it for a wager.

Cressida was trying not to feel excited. It was all so fascinating. She had seen in the light of the flames as she and her father had turned into the Manor drive, the earl carrying Annabelle away from the house in his arms. Now Annabelle's useless husband was dead. He had probably set the place on fire himself by knocking over the bed candle. What a marvelous heroine Annabelle made! How like an engraving in a novel she had looked with her hair streaming down her back and her face as pale as alabaster.

After they had reached the vicarage and she had supervised putting Annabelle to bed, Cressida lay awake for a long time, planning Annabelle's future. Cressida was too young and thought too little of herself to realize that she was in love with the earl, and wished to live out the romance she dimly felt she never could have, by organizing Annabelle's life.

Annabelle awoke late and sat up in bed, struggling to cope with all the horrible memories of the night. The sun was streaming in the bedroom window. It all seemed like a horrible dream. She got out of bed and looked about her. She had no clothes to wear. She thought sadly of her beautiful gown, now, no doubt reduced to ashes, and then shuddered to think that she could mourn a ballgown and not her husband.

Guy!

She hugged her shivering body as waves of shock and anger and grief passed through her.

The door opened, and Cressida stood there, surveying her guest with something like satisfaction. Oh, if the earl could only see his Annabelle with that romantic distress on her face! But in her usual practical way, she said, "I have brought you some clothes I hope will fit you. You must have some fresh air, eat a little, and then retire to bed again.

Try not to think of it. Papa and I will do all we can to help."

It was then that Annabelle began to cry in a lost dreary way. For the first time in her life, she felt without hope of any kind.

When she had finally dried her eyes, bathed her face, and dressed, Cressida said, "May I write to your parents, or relatives?"

"The cholera took my parents late last year," said Annabelle. "Such relatives as I do have are very poor and could not help."

"Then Mr. Carruthers' parents?"

"Dead, too, and such other family as he had disowned him this age."

"Oh," sighed Cressida happily. "Then you must leave things to us. I am sure the Earl of Darkwood will arrange all matters suitably for you."

Annabelle's face hardened. "I must tell you, Cressida, that had it not been for that fire, I would still not have been able to stay at the Manor. Guy lost it in a card game last night with the earl's friends."

"But you are a widow! No one can keep you to such an monstrous wager. Who won the Manor?"

"A Captain Jamieson, I believe."

"Then the earl must tell him to tear up that IOU. It is only fitting."

Annabelle smiled wanly. "I see you do not know about gambling debts. They must always be paid, no matter who is ruined in the process. Captain Jamieson has won a mortgaged, smoldering ruin. Even if he did hand it back to me, there is nothing I could do with it."

"Come downstairs and take a little breakfast,"

urged Cressida. "We will be able to see things more clearly as the day goes on."

Annabelle dutifully drank tea and ate a little toast. The vicar called her into his study.

"You must make your home with us for as long as you like, Mrs. Carruthers," he said gravely. "I have been discussing the matter with Cressida. If you will allow me, I will make the funeral arrangements. The Earl of Darkwood has kindly said he will meet all expenses."

"No! He cannot."

"My dear," said Mr. Knight, "I believe you have no choice, and you owe it to your poor husband to see he is decently buried."

Three days later, Annabelle followed her husband's body to the churchyard while the great bell in the Norman tower of the church tolled out the long strokes of the death knell. The earl was there with his friends but not his sister, who had returned to her own estates with her husband after the ball.

He was dressed in black mourning clothes and looked almost satanic, a formidable figure in the morning sunlight. Memories raced through Annabelle's mind as the coffin was lowered into the grave. Her mother saying sadly, "You must accept Mr. Carruthers's offer. We have very little money, and you would be off our hands. Such as we are not allowed to choose in marriage."

She remembered Guy collecting money at the wedding reception for he had bet his friends that she would not be wearing a wedding veil and had won. She remembered the honeymoon at one of Guy's gambling friend's country homes and how in that brief spell he had seemed to be genuinely in love with her; she had felt happy and confident that she would come to love him. But soon it was all over and Guy was drinking and gambling heavily. She had learned to avoid him when he was drunk, for the first time she had tried to remonstrate with him, he had beaten her, and his maudlin remorse the next day was almost as bad as the beating.

There was a simple funeral reception at the vicarage and then the earl spoke to Mr. Knight and approached Annabelle.

"I wish to talk to you in private, Mrs. Carruthers," he said. "The vicar says we may use his study."

Annabelle bowed her head in assent and walked into the study with him.

"Please sit down," said the earl, pulling out a chair for her. "Has your husband's lawyer been to see you?"

Annabelle looked bewildered. "I do not know the names of my husband's lawyers, and I assume all papers have been destroyed. But there should be some in our town house. I shall travel there shortly. I cannot go on being a burden on the vicar's household."

He held out a parcel. "These are items and clothing I took from your husband's body. As you know, Mr. Carruthers lost the Manor in play. I need hardly tell you about gambling debts, but if you wish, I shall try to get Captain Jamieson to forget the debt."

"I belive the manor was mortgaged to the hilt," said Annabelle. "I could not do anything to restore the building even if I had it back."

He surveyed her gravely. She was wearing a

black gown of Cressida's, and her hair was severely braided, and she was very white. And yet there was something about her, a softness, a femininity that made his pulses race as, say, Rosamund Clairmont never could. He gave himself a mental shake. He had more or less decided to ask Rosamund to marry him. He was an aristocrat who owed it to his ancient name and lands to marry well. Such was the way of the world. He had never-been in love and considered that emotion a transient thing. Marriage should be based on money and breeding.

But all in that moment, she looked younger than Rosamund and painfully vulnerable. He asked her about family, his face darkening as he learned she had no one on whom she could rely.

Despite all her grief and distress, Annabelle was aware of a sharp longing not to be an object of pity.

"I do have one very good friend in London, Matilda, Duchess of Hadshire," she said. "The duchess will help me come about. I have the town house to sell, and then I can repay you for the funeral arrangements."

"There is no reason to pay me anything," he said, almost angrily. "But I am glad you have such a powerful friend. You will be in sore need of her. Here is my card with my London address. Call on me should you need anything."

"You are very kind," said Annabelle stiffly.

"I am only doing my duty," he replied and then felt as if Annabelle had retreated from him to the other side of a great gulf.

"I shall leave you now," he said. "All my best wishes for your future."

Annabelle sat looking straight ahead as he left the room.

As soon as the door had closed behind him, she slowly opened the parcel. There was Guy's gold watch, which he had miraculously not pawned, sold, or gambled away, and one hundred pounds in notes. Annabelle turned them over. Notes, again! Men usually gambled in sovereigns. The owner of White's Club in St. James's would stay all night to clear up after the gamblers, for they often left gold spilled on the floor. The mysterious Mr. Temple must have had something to do with the money Guy had received. There was also a snuffbox and a handkerchief and a lucky rabbit's foot and a lucky penny. Then there was a small leather notebook, its pages stained and curled and smelling of brandy. She opened it. It was a diary of various bets. The last entry puzzled her. "Shall restore fortunes tonight thanks to T.," it said. "But he shall soon learn I will not betray m . . ." The rest was lost in a great stain. There was also her husband's clothes. The smell of brandy was dreadful, as if Guy had poured bottles of the stuff over himself.

All the ruin of Guy's life seemed to be there in that parcel of effects. She put them all away and tied up the parcel again, keeping the money back, for it would be used to pay her fare to London.

London!

Matilda would be there, and Matilda's sharp common sense would be like a breath of fresh air.

Matilda, Duchess of Hadshire, sat up in bed three days later and read a letter from Annabelle. So Guy was dead, she mused, and good riddance, too. Matilda longed to see Annabelle again. Annabelle was the only remaining person she could talk to about her disastrous marriage to the duke. Ladies normally did not talk of such things. It was a woman's place to be loyal to her husband at all times in speech and action. Matilda knew that she was a sore disappointment to her husband. He had married her because Matilda, with her delicate Dresden looks, was something he longed to add to his collection of objets d'art. Her forthright manner and honest speech had come as a shock to the fastidious duke. But one can hardly put a wife away in the cellar along with the other mistakes, vases that did not quite please the eye, paintings that no longer excited the aesthetic senses, and so Matilda was allowed a tolerable life so long as she wore the clothes he chose for her and spoke as little as possible. She would need to find some way to see Annabelle without her husband knowing about it, for he had forbidden her to visit the Carrutherses, claiming it was rumored that Carruthers had had a hand in the abduction of Emma, Comtesse Saint Juste. She could not defy him for he would set his valet, Rougement, on her; the brutal Rougement, who followed his master like a shadow and obeyed him as willingly as a dog. Matilda often thought Rougement was jealous of her.

She looked at the letter again. Annabelle planned to arrive the following week. Matilda bit her lip in vexation. Her husband held the purse strings and took a weekly inventory of her jewelry. Annabelle, Matilda knew, would be coming to a house without servants or food.

But the main thing was to get to see Annabelle. It should be quite simple. All she had to do was say she was making calls or driving in the park.

* * *

Annabelle arrived in London on a warm gray day. A thin drizzle was falling. She felt buffeted by the sounds of the streets, the rumble of the brewers' sledges, the clarion call of the coaches' horns, the postmen's bells, and all the street cries of London—"Fresh watercress"—"Fresh mackerels, ha' you maids"—"Bellows to mend"—and all the other multifarious cries of the great city. Guy's town house was tucked in a corner of Clarence Square, a thin dark building, looking crushed by its larger and more aristocratic neighbors.

Her unpacking did not take long; Cressida had given her clothes along with several bales of cloth to make new gowns. Annabelle looked bleakly around the dusty, unaired house. She threw back the shutters in all the rooms and then, before she started cleaning, she went to Guy's bedroom to look for papers. There was a desk in the corner. To her horror, it seemed to be packed with unpaid bills. She kept on searching and then, to her amazement, she found that Guy had actually made a will leaving everything to her. She took a note of the lawyer's address, planning to visit him as soon as possible to find out where she stood.

She looked at his clothes in the wardrobe. She would have to steel herself to sell them and to sell everything possible so that she might be able to exist for a short time. She would need to pay hard cash for food. No more credit.

By the end of the weary day, she felt more at peace than she had for a long time. She had worked hard, and the house was cleaned and aired. She had bought some mackerel from a street vendor for her supper and a loaf of bread from the bakers. She would not starve. She tried to think about her husband. She tried to mourn him, but all she could think of was that she would never hear his staggering footsteps on the stairs at night again, dread his fumbling hand on her bedroom door, or fear his rages.

The first week in London passed quickly. She managed to engage the services of a cleaning woman to do the "rough," but shrank from engaging proper servants who would have to be paid and fed. In the evenings she stitched diligently, transforming the bales of cloth that Cressida had given her into fashionable gowns and pelisses, all in dark colors, suitable for mourning. She gradually learned to do without servants, experiencing a feeling of triumph when she managed to heat water for a bath and fill it. The benefit of living alone was that she did not need to carry the coffin-like bath up to the bedroom, but could bathe by the kitchen fire.

Matilda arrived on a sunny afternoon and looked startled when Annabelle answered the door herself, her hair covered by a chintz cap and with a cotton apron over her gown.

Annabelle hugged her warmly and led her upstairs to the drawing room. As they sat down, Annabelle was acutely conscious of the contrast in their appearance. She was wearing what amounted to a servant's dress, but Matilda was wearing a dainty striped gown and had a chip straw bonnet on her head ornamented with silk flowers.

"I fear for you," said Matilda. "You cannot continue to live in the middle of fashionable London like some impoverished recluse. Oh, if only I could give you money. But Hadshire takes note of every jewel I have and every gown I wear. Tiresome man. You are lucky, Annabelle. A dead husband is a wondrous thing."

"Poor Guy," sighed Annabelle. "I still grieve, Matilda, and feel guilty for I did wish him dead so many times. Sometimes, I feel as if I had murdered him." She covered her face with her hands and began to cry. In a flurry of silks, Matilda darted across the room and knelt at her feet. "Hush, now," she said. "I did not mean to be so blunt. We will think of something. Never fear. Of course you did not murder your husband. He probably knocked over the bed candle. You know he had done that before."

Captain Jamieson and the Earl of Darkwood poked about the smoldering ruins of the Manor. "A mess, isn't it?" said the captain. "Demme, I wish I had never taken it on."

The earl peered out of a smoke-blackened window. "Fair piece of land," he said. "You have not done so badly. Is it safe to go upstairs?"

"I suppose so," said the captain doubtfully. "Keep to the left, though. The right side's nearly burnt away."

They climbed up cautiously. Some rooms above were blackened holes, the roof open to the sky, others were surprisingly intact.

"And here's where it all happened," said the earl, standing on the threshold of Guy's bedchamber.

"How can you tell?" asked the captain. "Looks like a great burnt-out shell to me."

"The smell, man, the smell. It still reeks of brandy." The earl poked at several empty blackened bottles with his stick. "Now how could anyone stay awake long enough to drink five whole bottles of brandy?"

"Probably didn't," said the captain laconically. "Probably evaporated in the fire."

"I think not. The seals on the bottles are broken. Do not walk on the floor. It is not safe!"

The earl continued to poke about with his cane but without venturing too far into the room. He lifted up a piece of charred bed hanging and lifted it to his nose. "Brandy, again," he said quietly. And then in a louder voice, "I'll take this ruin off your hands, if you like. The land adjoins mine, and I could run the two estates together."

Captain Jamieson looked at him with relief. "I say, that would be a great scheme. I've just been wondering what on earth to do with the place. Let's go back to Delaney and discuss it over a bottle."

"So long as it is not brandy," said the earl. "I don't think I want to smell brandy again."

He half listened to his friend's chatter as they walked home. He kept thinking about all that brandy. The room had been doused in brandy. Carruthers's clothes had reeked of brandy. He had a sudden vision of Mrs. Carruthers moving quickly about her husband's bedchamber as he lay in a drunken sleep, pouring brandy everywhere, even pouring it over her husband's body. And then what? Stand by the door with a lighted candle in her hand. Throw the candle into the room and walk quietly away. But why climb perilously down the wall in her nightgown when she could have pretended to have still been fully dressed when the fire started? Well, maybe that was clever of her. Very clever. She had not shed a tear at the funeral.

"We shall be back in town tomorrow," he realized the captain was saying. "Need a bit of life after the country, hey?"

"Yes," said the earl slowly, trying to banish that

picture of Annabelle setting out to kill her husband.

Annabelle read in the social columns that the Earl of Darkwood was in residence in his town house. She had felt guilty wasting money on a newspaper, but persuaded herself it was good for her to keep abreast of the news, although she had turned immediately to the social column. Would he marry Rosamund, she wondered. Or would some other heiress snatch him up before Rosamund arrived?

There came a thunderous knocking at the door. She threw down the newspaper and went to answer it. A squat, oily man stood there, flanked by two burly henchmen.

"Where is your mistress?" he asked.

"I am Mrs. Carruthers," said Annabelle coldly.

He handed her a grimy card. "And I am Silas Gadshaw, moneylender," he said. He put his hand in his pocket and drew out a sheaf of papers. "This here's the title deeds to this house. Your husband gave them to me against money he borrowed. Just learned he's dead so I come to take possession."

Annabelle looked at him in a dazed way.

"It cannot be true," she whispered.

"True enough."

"But you must give me time. I have nowhere to live."

"Sorry, madam, but I am taking possession now. The house and everything in it belongs to me." He leered at her. "I'll give you time to pack your belongings."

There was nothing Annabelle could do except obey. If she refused, he would take possession of the house by force. She let them into the hall and then went to her room and began to pack her trunks. There was the parcel of Guy's effects still reeking of brandy. She threw the parcel in the bottom of one of the trunks. The packing seemed to take an age. Her fingers were stiff as if with cold.

At last she was ready. One of the henchmen who seemed to have a softer heart than his master ran out into the street to fetch her a hack.

"Grosvenor Square," said Annabelle as she climbed into the carriage. There was only Matilda to go to now.

But at the Duke of Hadshire's imposing mansion, Annabelle began to realize that there was nowhere to go at all. The butler who opened the door surveyed her and her shabby trunks as if regarding an insect. She handed him her card and asked to see the duchess. He inclined his head and retreated into the house, leaving her standing on the steps. He went straight to the duke, who was dressing.

"What is it?" asked the duke, his pale eyes fastened on the intricacies of his cravat.

"A Mrs. Carruthers has turned up with her trunks asking for Her Grace."

"Then we need not trouble Her Grace with such a person. Tell this Mrs. Carruthers to go away. Her Grace is not available now or at any other time."

With great relish, the butler repeated the message word for word, except as if it came from the duchess and not the duke. He then slammed the door in Annabelle's face.

She stood there, shaking. No one wanted her. She could not even return to the vicarage, for Cressida had written to say that she and her father had gone to visit relatives in Bath.

Then she thought of the earl. He had asked her to come to him should she need help. So he would help her for he considered that his duty. And then what? She had no claim on the Darkwood family. She could not expect to be their pensioner for life. He was a man with the reputation of a rake. Perhaps she could offer herself. She was not a virgin. After her marriage to Guy, she should surely be able to tolerate the familiarities of the bedroom in return for food and lodging. She would lose her reputation, but one could not eat reputation or warm one's hands at it. If he took her as mistress, then it would give her a breathing space to find some sort of work.

A hack was clopping toward her around the square. She raised a hand and hailed it and gave the driver the Earl of Darkwood's address.

Chapter Five

THE EARL OF DARKWOOD was feeling like the very devil he was often reputed to be. His head was hot and heavy, and he was sure he was in for another bout of the fever that had plagued him on and off since his army days. The fact that he had been drinking heavily with his friends all afternoon had not helped.

He wondered what on earth had possessed him to return so easily to his earlier life of drinking and roistering. His time spent recently at Delaney now seemed, in retrospect, to be a haven of peace. He had agreed to meet his friends again that evening for a midnight curricle race to Box Hill.

Well, he would go and be damned to this fever. He stubbornly thought that if he ignored his illness, it would miraculously go away.

His butler, an ex-army servant who still looked like a veteran despite his expensive livery, appeared in the library and surveyed his master gloomily.

"There's a female and her traps a-standing on your lordship's doorstep, demanding to see you on a private matter."

The earl put a hand to his hot forehead and

groaned. What *had* he been doing that afternoon? It came and went in flashes. Had he picked up some doxy and invited her to his home?

"I think I can leave the matter to you, Barnstable. Send the doxy packing and say I made a mistake."

"Doesn't look to me like a doxy," said Barnstable. "Got a card. Name of Mrs. Carruthers."

"What?"

"You heard," said the butler with the easy informality born long ago on the battlefield between master and servant.

"The deuce. Show her in here. Has she got a maid with her or any other female?"

"Not as I could see."

"Then keep quiet about this and tell the other servants she never called and they've never seen her. Bring negus and some biscuits."

Barnstable returned downstairs to the doorstep. "Leave your bags there, mum," he said, "and come in quick before anyone sees you."

Annabelle followed him into the hall, a hall she noticed had not been swept for some time, and then up an uncarpeted staircase with unpolished steps. The banister was greasy under her hand.

She stood in the doorway of the library as Barnstable announced her. It was a large shadowy room with serried ranks of calf-bound books rising from floor to ceiling. The floor was covered in a jumble of books and magazines, riding crops, guns, cartridges, old game bags, and a few discarded clothes. A fire was struggling gamely to stay alight in a hearth nearly choked with ash.

Her heart misgave her as she surveyed the earl. He looked satanic. His eyes were glittering, his black hair was disheveled, and he was wearing a gaudy dressing gown over breeches and a shirt open at the neck.

"Sit down, Mrs. Carruthers," he ordered, "and keep quiet until Barnstable has brought you something to drink."

"It must seem very odd to you . . ." began Annabelle.

But he snapped, "Be quiet," and turned away from her, leaning his arm on the mantel and moodily kicking a smoldering log in the fireplace.

Barnstable returned with the negus and biscuits on a tray. He looked at the small console table beside Annabelle that was covered in magazines and newspapers and then swept them to the floor with one hand and placed the tray on it with the other.

The earl remained motionless until he had left and closed the door behind him. Then he turned and thrust his hands into the pockets of his dressing gown and looked at Annabelle.

"Well?" he demanded.

Annabelle half raised her glass to her lips and then put it down again. "I . . . I am come to put a proposition to you," she said. She felt sick with fright. The man she had known in the country had been more approachable, almost kind, not this wild and cruel-looking stranger. But he was a rake, she reminded herself, and she would hardly have dared to offer herself to a respectable gentleman.

"What have you to offer?" he asked, his green eyes insolently raking over her. He noticed she was wearing a fashionable gown of pink muslin with a pelisse of darker rose pink silk over it. Her eyes seemed enormous in her face, great, dark fathomless pools.

Annabelle grasped her hands tightly together. "Myself."

There was a long silence.

"In what capacity, may I ask?"

"As your mistress," said Annabelle desperately. "You see, I have nowhere else to go. Mr. Carruthers had drawn money from a moneylender and left the title deeds of the town house as security. The moneylender came this day to take possession."

"Then I suggest you return to the good vicar."

"He and his daughter have gone to Bath."

"What about the Duchess of Hadshire?"

Annabelle hung her head.

"Wouldn't see you, hey? Stand up!"

Annabelle got shakily to her feet, hanging onto the chair back for support. He walked around her.

"Yes, very fetching," he said. He put a hand to his head and groaned.

"What is the matter?" asked Annabelle. "Are you ill?"

He shook his head as if to clear it. "No, no. Sit down again. Drink your negus, and let me think."

He slumped down in a chair by the fire. Of course she might be a murderess, but he could not bring himself to think so. Perhaps Guy had deliberately brought about his own death. The earl could offer her money, but he had a strong feeling she would not take charity. He could pretend to take her on, set her up in a house, put a chaperon in, and then when he was feeling better, talk some sense into her. The obvious solution was for her to marry again. He would give her enough of a dowry to puff her off. He had discovered that the Manor possessed two good tenant farms, and the land was in excellent condition. With supervision and new farming methods, it would yield much more than it had ever done. Despite the ruin of the house, he had made a profitable investment. No use handing it back to her. She would not have enough money to bring the estate into shape. Best get rid of her as soon as possible.

"Yes," he said slowly. "I'll take your offer. I don't want you to stay here. I do not normally keep my ladies in my home."

Annabelle winced.

"I'll set you up in a place and get you staff. You'd better let me find some respectable female to live with you. I do not like to broadcast my amors about the town. You had better let me escort you to some genteel hotel until I can make arrangements. Now I think that is all, Mrs. Carruthers. Stay here and finish your wine while I dress." He rose to his feet and smiled at her. "I think we shall deal together extremely well."

A look of surprise crossed his face followed by bewilderment. He put out his hand to find something with which to support himself, gave a choked exclamation, and fell like a stone to the floor.

Annabelle ran and knelt beside him and then jumped to her feet and rang the bell. Barnstable came hurrying in.

"Your master," whispered Annabelle. "Is he dead? Please God, do not let him be dead."

Barnstable knelt down beside the earl, his wrinkled face against his master's chest, and then felt his forehead.

"Thought so," he said. "His lordship's got the fever again, mortal bad. Just leave him to me, ma'am, I've dealt with it many times afore."

Annabelle took a deep breath. She had burnt her boats. She was now the earl's mistress.

"I am staying here," she said firmly. "Summon the footmen to help your master to bed, and then the physician and I shall nurse him."

"We never has ladies here," said Barnstable mulishly.

"We cannot stand here arguing," said Annabelle. "Cannot you see how ill his lordship is? Do as you are told."

"Very well," said Barnstable, rising and ringing the bell. "But he didn't want no one knowing about you here, so you just tell the doctor you're his married cousin, see, and tell the other servants the same!"

"Oh, anything," said Annabelle.

Two footmen came in, and they and the butler carried the earl out. Annabelle followed them, but Barnstable turned in the doorway after the earl had been laid on his bed.

"You'd best be off while we strips him," he said. "The room along there has your traps in it. Stay and I'll call you when he's settled."

Annabelle walked off to where he had pointed and pushed open the door of a bedroom. It was dark and old-fashioned with a great four-poster bed. There was no fire, and it smelled of damp and disuse. She took off her bonnet and pelisse and then rang the bell. After about ten minutes, a housemaid scratched at the door and walked in. She was a cheeky elfin creature with an unruly mop of red hair showing under a grimy cap.

"I am Mrs. Carruthers," said Annabelle firmly. "His lordship's cousin. I shall be staying here to nurse him. I want this room cleaned and aired now and a fire lit. What is your name?"

"Margaret, mum."

"Very well, Margaret, go and get help or I shall come looking for you."

Margaret soon returned with two other equally slatternly-looking maids. Annabelle stood over them, making sure every inch of the room was dusted, a fire lit in the grate, and clean sheets spread before the fire to warm.

"Where is the housekeeper?" she demanded.

"Begging your parding, mum," said Margaret pertly. "We don't have none, the last one having been taken by the gin."

Annabelle looked at her thoughtfully. A servants' hall without rank or privilege was an unhappy, sloppy place. Barnstable appeared in the doorway. "Got his lordship to bed now, mum," he said. "The leech is on his way."

Instructing the maids to keep on working and polish what they had dusted, Annabelle followed Barnstable to the earl's bedroom.

"Oh, Barnstable," she sighed. "This is no way for a sickroom to be. Fetch the maids along here, and set them to work."

She drew a chair up to the side of the bed and felt the earl's forehead. It was burning hot. He tossed and mumbled. "Get me cologne or rose water," ordered Annabelle. "Also a basin of clean water and washing cloths."

The maids worked diligently as Annabelle gently bathed and washed the earl's fevered face. She was just giving Barnstable instructions to lay straw down on the street outside to muffle the sound of passing carriages when the doctor was ushered in.

She retired to a corner of the room while the doctor unpacked cupping glasses and got to work to bleed the patient.

Annabelle felt uneasy. She did not like the practice of bleeding, feeling it often weakened a sick patient too much, but did not like to say so.

When the doctor was finished, he drew her outside. "This is a bottle of mercury," he said. "Give him some drops of it mixed with brandy every four hours."

Annabelle took the mercury. The doctor said he would call in the morning. After he had gone, Annabelle slipped the mercury into her reticule and when Barnstable, who had followed her from the room to listen to the doctor's instructions, came in with a decanter of brandy, she waited until he had gone and drank a glass of it herself. She had read an article in a ladies' magazine that claimed that the taking of mercury was dangerous. Something in her told her the magazine article was right.

The earl shouted something incoherent, and she soaked a cloth in warm scented water, wrung it out, and placed it on his forehead. His eyes opened, and he looked at her wildly. His nose twitched, and he said quite clearly, "Brandy. Are you going to murder me as well?" Then he relapsed into unconsciousness again.

Annabelle frowned. What had he meant? He was delirious, of course. He must have smelled the brandy on her breath. But did he think she had murdered Guy? Brandy. Guy's clothes had been soaked in brandy. Her hand bathing his forehead trembled. Poor Guy. Had the loss of the Manor been the final straw? Had he poured brandy over himself like that mad squire she had read about and set himself alight?

But what she had learned through Guy and his gambling friends was that they seemed driven to lose, not to win, so losses, however great, did not matter so long as they could find some money somewhere, somehow, to continue. And where had Guy found the money? He must have been given that hundred pounds after the card room was closed. Temple. When she was finally settled somewhere, she would need to seek out Mr. Temple and ask him a few questions.

She remained by the earl's bed throughout the night unaware that by doing so she had made Barnstable a devoted admirer. The grizzled butler at last coaxed her to go and lie down. "I shall call you if he gets worse, mum," he said. "Reckon you'd nurse him better if you had a little sleep."

"Thank you, Barnstable, you are most kind. Tell me, why is it that this house is so badly run? His lordship's home in the country was in perfect order."

"He hasn't lived here, not for a long time," said Barnstable. "Brought me back from the wars to be his butler but I ain't a good hand with the maids. Can't tell good from bad, and the housekeeper that was in residence here let everything go to rack and ruin."

"I do not want to take too much on myself," said Annabelle, "but I feel it would be better for his lordship's health were we to engage a good housekeeper as soon as possible. It was kind of you to bring me supper, but the food was disgracefully bad. Who is the cook?"

"Well, there ain't one as yet," said Barnstable.

"Mayhap when you've rested, mum, we could try to get one. Meanwhile, the maids will do their best."

"Very well," said Annabelle, rising wearily to her feet. "I think a good plain cook to begin with, someone expert in the preparation of invalid dishes. I am quite a good cook myself. I shall inspect the kitchens later."

"On your own head be it," said the butler gloomily.

Annabelle was to find out the reason for his gloom after she had had a few refreshing hours sleep and made her way downstairs. The kitchen was appalling, a mess of grease and dirty dishes and an old open fireplace with blackened pots hanging over it.

She retreated upstairs and put on one of her old gowns and an apron and cap and descended again, prepared to do battle. She sent Barnstable out to search the employment agencies for temporary servants to help with the initial cleaning and also to find a cook and a housekeeper. Then when she had finally seen the army of newly hired servants scrubbing and cleaning, she interviewed a long line of prospective cooks and housekeepers, finally settling on two sensible middle-aged women from the country.

Then she lined up the resident staff and gave them a scalding lecture on the benefits of personal cleanliness. New print dresses and white aprons and caps were to be ordered for the maids and new clean linen for the footmen and for Barnstable. She created new ranks for the servants, first footman, second footman, under butler, housemaids, chambermaids, between-stair maids, and scullery maids. Any maid of low rank showing herself to be hard-working and diligent would quickly rise in the ranks, said Annabelle, and then retired to the sickroom to look after her patient.

She had two footmen carry the earl to a temporary daybed while she stripped his bed and had clean lavender-scented, aired sheets placed on it. The earl's bedroom was now spotlessly clean, she noticed with satisfaction.

Annabelle was grateful for the nursing and the reorganization of the earl's household. It gave her little time to think of herself or her predicament.

The earl's fever broke in the middle of the night, and Annabelle sent up a grateful prayer of thanks. It was only when Barnstable relieved her at the bedside and she made her way to her own bedroom that she realized her own troubles were soon about to begin. As the earl's supposed married cousin, she was respected by the servants. Soon they would know that she was nothing more than his mistress, and she was sure they would, with the exception of Barnstable, treat her with insolence.

When she arose again, she entered his room carrying the daily newspapers. He was lying propped against the pillows, and his green eyes were clear and bright and full of intelligence.

"I am come to read to you," said Annabelle calmly. She sat down beside the bed.

"Before you begin," said the earl, "you must realize, Mrs. Carruthers, that I have but a vague memory of your arrival here. Was it a fevered dream or did you offer to become my mistress?"

"Yes," said Annabelle calmly.

"The deuce. I must have been mad. Never mind. I shall find you somewhere to live. What a confounded bore it all is."

"Hardly loverlike," commented Annabelle.

"Love is one thing, mistresses another," he said testily.

Annabelle flushed. But she was used to insults and sneers from Guy and did not expect men to behave any better. Knights on white chargers were for dreams and novels. In real life, thought Annabelle, men were little better than petulant children.

She reminded herself sternly that he was still ill and settled herself to read to him.

He lay back in bed and listened to her quiet even voice and felt a strange peace steal over him. His bed was cool and fresh, and there was a scent of flowers in the air. He opened his eyes. Beyond Annabelle on a small table was a vase of spring flowers.

A footman entered with a tray. The earl struggled up against the pillows. "If I eat anything out of that kitchen of mine," he said crossly, "I shall have a relapse."

"I took it upon myself to hire a cook," said Annabelle, "and a housekeeper and some temporary servants to put the kitchen in order. I hope you do not mind. Barnstable will present you with the accounts when you are feeling better."

"No," said the earl dryly, "it is a new experience for me to have my money spent on practical things rather than gowns and jewelry."

He drank some excellent chicken broth while Annabelle continued to read, but with part of her mind racing. He was used to mistresses; women whose whole role in life was to be frivolous and charming. How on earth could she even begin to match up?

After his light meal, he said, "Put away the newspapers, and ring for Barnstable."

Annabelle did as she was bid. When the butler arrived, the earl said, "Get my London agent here, Struthers, at the double. I have arrangements to make. And get me pen and ink and paper. I want a footman to take a letter to my aunt, Miss Davenant."

"Very good, my lord," said Barnstable. "Feeling better?"

"Yes, you old rogue."

"You have Mrs. Carruthers here to thank for that," said Barnstable. "Regular Trojan, her were, nigh killing herself sitting up all night; not to mention getting the servants in order."

"I am deeply grateful to you," said the earl to Annabelle. "You may retire now and rest. But do not leave the house. No one must see you here."

Annabelle rose and curtsied and left.

"Well," demanded the earl. "What are you doing hanging about, Barnstable? I gave you orders."

"I just wanted for to say," said Barnstable stiffly, "that Mrs. Carruthers has made this a real home and in such a short space of time. Will she be staying?"

"No, she will most definitely not be staying and would not be here had I not fallen ill with the fever. Go about your duties."

"You ought to get married, so you ought," said the butler and closed the door quickly before the astonished earl could reply.

And that, thought the earl cynically, was probably what Mrs. Carruthers was about. He was used to being pursued. Ambitious mothers and their daughters had even pursued him as far as Spain.

Mistress, indeed! Still, he should not be too hard on her. What else could she do in life except try to marry again?

When his agent arrived, he told that gentleman to find a house for a certain Mrs. Carruthers. "No," he snapped to the agent's unspoken question, "I am not setting up another lightskirt. This is an indigent relative, so make it a respectable address suitable for two ladies."

"Sir Alexander Baxter has a property to rent. Was let down. Thought he had rented it for the Season. Nice little place in Burton Street, right near the Green Park. Can get it cheaper than he was originally asking."

"Sounds all right. Try to secure it today, and return to me as soon as you have the keys."

The earl's next visitor was his aunt. Miss Davenant was a faded spinster. The earl had never really thought about her much. She turned up at various family reunions, always the forgotten relative. She was tall with an amiable, indeterminate face. Her clothes looked as if they had been thrown on her by an angry lady's maid. She was all bits. Bits of jewelry, threads hanging from her skirts, and covered in a multitude of little colored scarves. She was in her fifties and had a face like that of a rather intense sheep. Her white hair was tightly curled and of the texture of wool. Among the paraphernalia dangling from her wrist—parasol, fan, smelling bottle on a leather strap, was a chintz workbag from which strands of pale wool hung down.

After the greetings were over, the earl said, "I want you to help me and to be discreet about it. How would you like to earn some money?"

Miss Davenant blinked. No one asked gently-bred females if they would like to earn money. Poor relations such as herself were expected to starve between family visits.

"Earn money?" she echoed faintly.

"Yes, I am in an awkward situation. A Mrs. Carruthers, who lived at the Manor, which adjoins Delaney, has fallen on hard times and came to me for help. I was stricken of the fever before I could make arrangements. She is here in this house."

Miss Davenant looked at him with her mouth open. Then she said faintly, "But that is most improper. Her reputation is ruined."

"Not if we all keep quiet, it isn't. Now I plan to take a house for her. She is very pretty and will soon marry again. She is in mourning, husband died recently, so she won't want to go jauntering about. I will pay you generously to be a companion to her until she gets on her feet. You need money, don't you?"

"You always were a blunt boy," said Miss Davenant. She felt she should reproach him for offering a gentlewoman money—and to look after some female who was obviously no better than she should be! But she thought of her tiny, cramped apartment where the sun never seemed to penetrate, of the loneliness of her days, of all the years of trying to make ends meet and keep up appearances, while the earl studied her curiously. He had never really known her, he thought, this faded aunt who sat so quietly in the corner of family drawing rooms as if she hoped to pass unobserved. He should have done something about her finances before, he thought ruefully. One always assumed that someone else was doing something about it.

"Before you speak," he said, "I would like to make you an allowance on a permanent footing. Meet this Mrs. Carruthers first. If you do not wish to be her companion, rest assured, you will still be provided for."

"I thought you were a rake," said Miss Davenant in childlike wonder.

"I was very wild in my youth," said the earl, ringing the bell, "and it seems as if the reputation I gained then will be with me to the grave."

A footman entered, and he asked for Mrs. Carruthers to attend him.

Miss Davenant looked at the door tremulously. She was sure she was being asked to cast a veil of respectability over the earl's mistress. As a lady, she should refuse. But a new, harder voice in her head was telling her that she was sick of trying to live on gentility. Whoever walked through that door represented comfort and hot meals and servants. It was very generous of dear Charles to offer to pay her an allowance. But she did not know him at all well and if she refused to companion this Mrs. Carruthers, perhaps he might lose his temper with her. Gentlemen were very testy, thought Miss Davenant.

The door opened, and Annabelle came in. She was wearing a black gown, simply and stylishly made. Her hair was neatly braided on top of her head, and her eyes were large and strangely innocent. Why! She's little more than a child, thought Miss Davenant.

The earl introduced his aunt and then said in a level voice, "my agent is finding a house for you, Mrs. Carruthers. My aunt, should she decide to undertake the job, would be prepared to act as your chaperon. Perhaps you ladies might like to retire to discuss the matter?"

Miss Davenant had dithered all her life. But for once she made up her mind on the spot. "If Mrs. Carruthers is willing," she said, "then I should deem it an honor to be her companion."

Annabelle looked at the faded and respectable lady in surprise. She thought it monstrous of the earl to coerce what was obviously a poor relative into chaperoning his mistress. She hesitated and then recognized the desperate appeal in Miss Davenant's eyes. Here was someone else who needed money badly.

"Thank you, Miss Davenant," she said quietly. "I am sure we shall deal together extremely well."

"Then take Miss Davenant off and give her some refreshment," said the earl, stifling a sigh of relief.

What it was to have money, he thought cynically as both ladies left. All he had to do now was to let Mrs. Carruthers live for a few weeks on his charity and then tell her he had no interest in her as a mistress and that he would supply her with a dowry. By the Little Season she would be able to attend a few functions in half mourning, and he himself would look about for a suitable husband for her. He felt quite a glow of self-righteousness.

Chapter Six

A WEEK HAD FLOWN past since the earl's recovery from his fever, a week of bustle and change and arrangements. Annábelle had inspected her new home in Clarence Square in the company of Miss Davenant. It was a pretty house with a saloon and morning room on the ground floor, dining room and drawing room on the first floor, three bedchambers on the second, and bedrooms in the attics for the servants.

Butler, housekeeper, cook, footman, and three maids had all been hired. All Annabelle needed to do was to pack and leave the earl's town house on the morrow for her new home. The earl had been distant and remote. All his dealings with her had been businesslike. Annabelle tried not to think of the day when she would be his mistress in body as well as name. She was packing her trunks when she found the parcel of Guy's clothes lying in the bottom of one of them. The smell of brandy was still strong. She opened the parcel and took out the clothes. She would give them to Barnstable to sell or throw away, whichever he wanted to do. But as the reek of stale brandy assaulted her nostrils, she suddenly remembered that brief moment before the ball when Guy had held her hands and told her about the letter he had left for her.

How could she have forgotten that? But the secret place in the paneling was probably a charred ruin like the rest of his bedchamber. But what was in that letter? Guy's death had been such a shock. She had not had time to think clearly. There was that hundred pounds. She still had a good deal of that money left and intended to keep it as security. But how had he come by it? When he had approached her at the dance for the money he had given her, he obviously had none left. So some time after leaving her and finding the card room locked up, he must have borrowed the money from someone. Who? Mr. Temple's fair and foppish face rose before her mind's eye.

When Emma was abducted, she had been on the road to visit her, Annabelle, and Guy had not only suggested the visit but had arranged the exact time. And Guy had come into a lot of money.

Annabelle felt a stab of fear. What *was* in that letter? If there was something in it which damned Guy himself as a traitor then she, by dint of being married to him, would appear guilty as well. Instead of throwing away the clothes, she carefully parceled them up again and placed them in the bottom of the trunk and went in search of Lord Darkwood.

She found the earl sitting at a desk in his library. He looked up as she came in. His eyes had a guarded, wary expression. "Yes, Mrs. Carruthers?" he asked.

Annabelle twisted a cambric handkerchief in her fingers, suddenly shy of him.

"I would beg a favor," she said.

He waited, looking at her curiously.

"I am anxious to have a last look around the Manor as soon as possible," said Annabelle.

"Indeed?" He threw down his pen. "You sold such effects as had survived the fire, did you not?"

"Yes, and gave that money to Mr. Knight for safekeeping. It was very little, or rather there was very little left after I had paid off the servants and a few remaining bills."

"So why do you wish to return?"

"Sentimental reasons, my lord."

"Fustian. You are not returning to your ancestral home, but to a damp, ugly building your husband bought some two years ago. The truth, Mrs. Carruthers."

Annabelle decided to tell half the truth. "I have always been uneasy in my mind about my husband's death," she said. "Yes, he was very drunk when he left your ball. But his clothes were soaked in brandy. The cellars were nearly empty, and I am sure he did not have time to go down before the fire to get the few remaining bottles. I wish to have another look at what is left of his bedchamber."

The earl's green gaze was unreadable. She half hoped he would tell her firmly that she was talking nonsense, that Guy had said something before he died, something about having started the fire by accident, but he said calmly, "Very well. I have some business affairs at Delaney. I have bought the Manor from Captain Jamieson, and the builders are already at work on it." He saw Annabelle blanche, and his interest quickened. "We shall leave tomorrow morning. My aunt may take up residence in Clarence Square and await our return."

"Thank you," said Annabelle faintly.

"Is there anything else?"

"N-no."

"Then you may leave me. I have much work to do."

Annabelle curtsied and walked out of the room, her heart thudding. They would be traveling together, and she would be able to get to know him better. If only they could become friends, then her situation would not be quite so hard.

She spent the afternoon at her husband's lawyers where she received a very cool reception, Guy having owed them money when he died. There were no secret assets, no hidden jewels, no stocks or shares: her spendthrift husband had made no provision for her. "I wonder if he even troubled to make a will," said Annabelle bitterly.

The elderly lawyer gave her a tired look. "You should be thankful, Mrs. Carruthers, that you do not have young children."

Children! thought Annabelle shakily as she left the lawyers. Guy, in his uglier moods, had called her barren. But what if the fault had lain with Guy? Then any children she had by the earl would be bastards. If only such a thing could be prevented. Men, she knew, could wear a condom, that contraceptive device invented in the previous century supposedly by a Colonel Cundum. But they only bothered to wear one when consorting with prostitutes and so avoid getting the pox, or so Guy had told her. Perhaps Matilda might know of some way in which a female could avoid becoming pregnant. But Matilda was no longer a friend. Matilda had turned her away.

Barnstable let her into the earl's house. The one thing that pleased Annabelle in her misery was the transformation of the house. It was clean and polished and smelled of beeswax and fresh flowers. The maids in their new dresses looked smart and efficient, although Annabelle feared that when the novelty of discipline wore off, they would soon return to their lazy ways. The maids' outfits had been made in a very short time, and she hoped the earl would not find the seamstress's bill too steep. But one always had to pay a lot more to have something made up quickly.

As usual, the earl did not dine with her. A meal was served to her in the drawing room while the earl ate in solitary state in the dining room. She wondered gloomily if this pattern would continue after she took up her duties as his mistress; if there was to be no intimacy other than sex between them.

At eight o'clock she was sitting sewing in her room when she heard a great commotion outside the house. Her window overlooked the front of the house. She went to it and drew back the curtains and looked down. There were three carriages full of bucks and bloods and their doxies.

She swung around as Barnstable entered the room. "Dear, oh dear," he said. "Quite like old times. When the master had the fever afore he was struck down with it, he was drinking hard in the clubs, and he must have invited all these wastrels to a party. Best lock your door, mum, till we gets rid o' them."

After he had left, Annabelle did as he had bidden her and tried to take up her sewing again. But the noise from downstairs was enormous. When she was his mistress, would she be expected to preside over such gatherings? What did these women do?

No one seemed to be coming up as far as the bedchambers. After an hour, she unlocked the door and crept along the passage to the landing. She leaned over the banisters. Two couples were dancing to a tune played on the mandolin by a drunken guest. The women's rouged faces were slack with drink. The men fondled their breasts as they danced. One man suddenly bore his partner down to the floor and mounted her. The other couple cheered and called to the rest of the company who spilled out into the hall to cheer the amorous couple on to further efforts. The earl was among them. He suddenly looked up and saw Annabelle at the top of the stairs and frowned and waved his hand in dismissal. She retreated to her room and locked the door and sat down with her legs shaking. What had she done?

At least her life with Guy had had some shreds of respectability.

Downstairs the earl surveyed his cavorting guests in disgust. The riots and parties that had amused him in his youth seemed appalling now. He opened the street door and began to usher his guests, some of them half clad, out into the street.

When the last had gone, he looked about at the glasses and bottles and mess with a scowl. In that moment he realized just how much Annabelle had changed the house. What on earth could she be thinking, and why on earth hadn't she stayed in her room?

He mounted the stairs and knocked on her door and called out, "It is I. Darkwood. Open the door."

He heard the key turn in the lock, and then Annabelle stood there, her eyes lowered.

"I told you to stay in your room," he said harshly. "What if someone had seen you?"

Annabelle kept her eyes lowered. "I am sorry," she said, "but I felt I must accustom myself to your way of life, to the ways of a mistress and . . ."

"I shall not expect you to behave like a trollop," he said harshly. "Such an affair will not happen again. Go to sleep. We leave at seven."

Annabelle curtsied, her eyelashes still lowered.

He turned away, furious with her, furious at himself. To hell with her. Soon she would be his pensioner, and he need never see her again. He would urge his aunt to take her about during the Little Season and to make sure she met suitable gentlemen, but he himself would concentrate on his own marriage plans.

Annabelle had dreaded the thought of being confined in a closed carriage with him on the journey. She felt as if a veil had been torn from her eyes. He was indeed a rake. But she found herself alone. He rode outside the carriage, and when they stopped for the night at a posting inn, he had his meals served to him in a private parlor, leaving her to dine in solitary splendor in her own private parlor. It was late when they arrived in Upper Chipping. Annabelle was not destined to stay at Delaney. He took rooms for her at the local inn and then rode off, saying he would call on her in the morning and take her to the Manor.

She lay awake for a long time, wondering what was going to happen to her. The earl was hard and remote, a stranger. How could she cope with the intimacies of a stranger? Guy had loved her in his fashion and that love had sustained her through the drunken rows and beatings and debt and humiliation. She turned her face into the pillow and cried for Guy, mourned him, for the very first time, falling asleep at last, weary with grief.

The earl arrived just as she was finishing breakfast. The day was fine and sunny, and he drove her in an open carriage out along the leafy lanes to the Manor. Builders were busy at work. The earl helped Annabelle down and then walked with her into the house. "I had better assist you," he said. "The building is still unsafe."

"I would rather be alone," said Annabelle determinedly. "If you do not mind."

"I shall escort you to your husband's room and leave you with your ... er ... grief, Mrs. Carruthers."

They walked silently up the stairs until they reached Guy's bedroom. Annabelle stood in the doorway.

"Do not venture in," cautioned the earl. "You may fall through the floor."

He turned and went down the stairs. Annabelle waited, not knowing that the earl had only gone as far as the first landing and was waiting as well. Her eyes flew to the far wall. It was charred black, but perhaps the spring that operated the secret panel still worked. She inched her way around the edge of the room, hoping that if the floor did give way, she could hang onto something on the walls like, say, one of the sconces or the mantelpiece.

The earl, who had darted quietly back up the stairs, stood just outside the door, looking round it, watching her, forcing himself not to rush forward for he was sure that any minute the floor would give and she would plunge to her death.

He saw her remove her gloves and press on something on the charred paneling. There was a click, and a section of the paneling swung open. Annabelle took out a sealed letter and slipped it into her reticule.

He moved away quietly and retreated downstairs, but listening all the time to make sure she was safe. When he heard her step on the stairs, he began to mount again as if he had been down in the hall all the time.

Annabelle started at the sight of him and clutched her reticule tightly to her bosom.

"Well?" he demanded.

"I beg your pardon?" Annabelle's eyes were very dark in her white face.

"Have you any idea as to how your husband met his death?"

Annabelle shook her head.

"There were brandy bottles," he said, "empty, in one corner of the room. They have been removed. Did he have them sent up from the cellars?"

"I do not think so," said Annabelle. She wanted to tell him, to tell someone, about the mysterious Mr. Temple. But if Mr. Temple had paid Guy for something criminal then perhaps she would be implicated in that crime. Justice was notoriously cruel to wives. A woman had been hanged only the other day because her husband had tortured and killed one of their maids. Although it was evident to Annabelle reading the evidence that the woman had been too terrified of her brutal husband to do anything to help the girl, she, too, was found guilty. Better to read the letter first.

They walked down the stairs together. The earl said curtly that he had to speak to the builders, and Annabelle said she would wait outside the front of the house.

She waited until he had turned a corner of the house and then walked away across the lawn to the shade of a cedar tree and took out the letter and broke open the half-melted seal. The paper was stiff and yellow from the heat of the fire, but the words were legible.

"My dear wife," she read, "I am writing this in a sentimental moment. I am sure I shall come about. But should anything happen to me, I swear on my mother's grave I am not a traitor. They gave me money to help in the abduction of the Comtesse Saint Juste. It was a joke, they said, and they had no intention of harming her. I knew they were traitors afterward. Now they are back again, and I need the money. But I am cleverer than they, and after a few days, I shall report them to the authorities. What can they do to me?

"But I saw a rook today and the bird looked at me oddly, almost like a human. I felt it was an omen. Should anything happen to me, my sweeting, rest assured I am not a traitor and that, poor husband as I am, I love you. Guy."

Annabelle's hands trembled. Had "they" come for him in the night, poured brandy over his sleeping body, and set the room alight?

She saw the earl rounding the corner of the house and stuffed the letter in her reticule and walked toward him.

He looked at her curiously but only said that they should set out for London immediately.

The earl was determined to see that letter. But when they stopped at a posting house for the night, he noticed Annabelle kept her reticule firmly attached to her wrist.

He awoke at four in the morning and listened to

the silence of the inn. He swung his long muscular legs out of bed and pulled on his dressing gown. He would creep into Annabelle's room and take a quick look at that letter. He was consumed with curiosity. He was beginning to think, more and more, that Guy Carruthers had been murdered.

He made his way to her room and gently tried the door. It was locked. He stood frowning, and then he remembered that one key to one door in the inn usually fitted the others. He returned to his own room and took the key from the door and then fitted it gently into the lock of Annabelle's bedroom door. There was a slight click, and the door swung open.

He moved softly into the room. The curtains were drawn back and moonlight streamed across the bed. Annabelle looked very young and defenseless in sleep.

Her reticule was lying on a chair beside the bed. He drew open the strings and felt inside.

"Who is there?" Annabelle's voice, sharp with fear.

He dropped the reticule and swung around. "It is only I, Darkwood."

"What do you want?" Annabelle struggled up against the pillows.

He smiled down at her in the moonlight. "You forgot to kiss me good night," he said.

Annabelle's heart plummeted like a stone. It was bound to happen sooner or later, she thought dismally. She had offered herself to him. He had merely come to take her up on her offer.

"It . . . it . . . is very late," she said pathetically. "Can it not wait until tomorrow?"

"My dearest, I thought you offered to be my mistress."

"Yes, so I did," said Annabelle miserably. "Very well, I shall kiss you." She screwed her eyes shut and puckered up her lips.

She shivered as she sensed rather than saw him leaning over her. Then his lips were against hers, hard and commanding. What happened next shocked them both. Annabelle's body seemed to leap into flame. The earl felt his senses whirling as his kiss grew deeper. His hand slid up her back to caress her neck under the heavy weight of her tumbling hair. He stretched out on the bed next to her, feeling the softness of her breasts against his chest. He moved away from her a little, and his hand slid down the neck of her nightgown and took possession of one full, rounded breast, and she moaned faintly against his mouth.

And then a little sharp cold thought entered his brain. He had no intention of seducing Annabelle Carruthers or becoming involved in any messy liaison. He stood up abruptly and said in a husky voice, "It is late."

Annabelle watched, wide-eyed, as he strode from the room.

Her body was aching and trembling and craving more kisses. Damn the man! He was a devil to arouse her so. The dreary fact that it all would mean nothing to him brought tears to her eyes. Now she was really frightened of him.

She lay awake for a long time, finally falling into a heavy sleep around dawn. That was when the earl returned to her room and took the letter. He carried it over to the window and read it carefully before returning it to her reticule and drawing the strings tight again.

He returned to his room and sat down in a chair.

It appeared Guy Carruthers had been working for the French. That Annabelle did not know anything about it was clear from the letter. It had happened after the ball. The traitor or traitors could not have been at that ball, for he had known everyone there with the exception of the Clairmonts, and they were surely above suspicion.

And then he remembered the supper room and being amused at the sight of his sister, unusually flirtatious, with a foppish young man. He had not remembered him and had asked who he was and learned that he was a stranger who had been staying at the inn. Temple, that was it. A Mr. Temple, who had stopped him in the village street and had spoken about the ball and had obviously been hoping for an invitation. He would need to go to the authorities in London with what he knew and see if this Mr. Temple could be taken for questioning, but he would need to make sure Annabelle was not arrested as well. Like Annabelle, he suddenly realized the wife was often found out to be as guilty as the husband, even if there were no proof.

To Annabelle's relief, the earl continued to ride outside the carriage and barely looked at her. To her even greater relief, he ordered the carriage to take her straight to Clarence Square.

Annabelle was welcomed by Miss Davenant. "Such a pretty house," she said, "and everything in the first style of comfort. So kind of Darkwood. I never thought of him as being a *kind* gentleman before."

Annabelle, too, before the episode in the posting inn, had had a tiny hope that the earl did not really mean to take her as his mistress, however that hope had now died. But how could he embroil his respectable aunt in such a ploy? Was that faded gentle-woman supposed to remain deaf and blind while he cavorted with her in her bedchamber?

But as Miss Davenant prattled on about the misery of her straitened circumstances, Annabelle began to believe that the earl knew his aunt would do anything for money and turn a blind eye when required. She was also sure that as yet Miss Davenant knew nothing of her disgraceful arrangement with the earl.

To her surprise, the earl did not put in an appearance during the following week. Or the week after that.

The earl had returned to Upper Chipping. The landlord of the Crown had given him the interesting information that Mr. Temple had called for five bottles of brandy in the small hours of the morning. The earl then rode to his sister's house and asked her if she still had Mr. Temple's card and to furnish him with the address.

Lady Trompington surrendered the card reluctantly. She often dreamed of Mr. Temple and of dancing with him at some ball.

The earl studied the address. Curzon Street, a good enough address in a way, but Mayfair could still house a great many parvenus.

On his return to London, he went to Horse Guards and laid what he knew about Mr. Temple and the death of Guy Carruthers before his old military commanders. He explained Annabelle's innocence and repeated the contents of that letter, word for word. One of the elderly generals facing him sighed and said, "We thought we had seen an end of this treachery. What could Carruthers have done for them anyway?"

"He was a gambler," said the earl, "and gambled with some of the top-ranking military. I assume the French were after the usual thing. They want to rescue their emperor from the island and carry him back to Paris in triumph. So they need to know the strength of the guard on him, when the guard is changed, the names of the officers of the guard, and which ones, home on leave, are liable to be vulnerable to blackmail or bribery. No one took Carruthers seriously, a bit of a wastrel, but a good fellow, that sort of thing. It is my belief he could have gained quite valuable information. I suggest you lend me two officers, and I shall take Temple myself."

"Take six at least," said the general. "He might manage to escape you."

Mr. Temple was preparing to go out. It was two in the afternoon, a fashionable hour to rise from bed. He lived in an apartment on top of a tall building in Curzon Street, near Shepherd Market. Curzon Street, despite all the aristocratic names that dwelt in it, still had a raffish air, as if the ghosts of the revelers from the old Mayfair still haunted it. Mr. Temple did not have a servant. He lived economically, all money he gained from his spying activities being lodged safely in Coutts Bank. Unlike other traitors, he did not betray his country for money, but for the feeling of power the secrecy of his life gave him. It made him feel important when he ingratiated his way into ton parties, to survey the gilded throng and think that when Emperor Napoleon was restored, they would soon all be marching to the guillotine. He was used to living dangerously and had developed a sort of sixth sense.

He was all at once sharply aware of danger. He

heard shuffling footsteps on the stairs and slowly took out a pistol, primed it, and stood facing the door.

The door swung open but it was only the housekeeper who looked after "her gentlemen," the men who rented the apartments in the building. He smiled and lowered the pistol. "I brought you a lamb chop and some porter," said the housekeeper, putting a tray down on the table. Mr. Temple almost laughed aloud at his fears. It should have dawned on him that it was odd the housekeeper did not make any remark about the pistol which he was now laying down on a side table.

She left the door open, and he went to close it just as the earl, followed by three officers, marched into the room. The other three were guarding the front entrance.

"What is this?" blustered Mr. Temple. "How dare . . . ?"

"I charge you in the king's name," said the earl, "with the murder of Mr. Guy Carruthers and with being a traitor to England."

"Fustian," said Mr. Temple, turning pale. "What proof have you?"

"Guy Carruthers left a letter for his wife," said the earl. "It incriminates you." It had not, in fact, but the earl was sure that Mr. Temple would believe him. "You will come with us."

One of the officers bound Mr. Temple's wrists. He was led down the stairs and out into a carriage. Where were they taking him? He must get help.

Lord Darkwood had instructions to take Mr. Temple to a military barracks in Chelsea. There he would be questioned so that they could find out the names of the other traitors. It was all to be done quietly, secretly, the authorities believing that a public trial would be bad for the morale of the country.

Mr. Temple's apartment was searched from top to bottom, but nothing incriminating was found.

He was locked in a small room and interrogated by the earl and two officers. He stubbornly protested his innocence and demanded the services of a lawyer.

The earl drew the officers outside the cell and said, "Leave him alone without food and water. He will talk soon enough."

Left to his own devices, Mr. Temple fought down rising waves of panic. It was not his fault. His employers had bungled, and bungled badly by choosing such a dangerously blabber-mouthed tool as Carruthers. He took off his coat and began to pick feverishly at the lining. There between lining and cloth he found a small notebook and pencil, and four guineas. He wrote a letter on a page of the notebook and went to the bars of his cell and looked out into the fading light. A sentry was parading up and down.

"Hist!" The sentry came to the barred window and looked at Mr. Temple curiously.

"If you take this letter to the gentleman whose name I have written on the other side," said Mr. Temple urgently, "he will reward you. Here are four guineas for you. Quickly. Before we are seen."

"What's it about," said the soldier suspiciously. He turned the paper this way and that.

Guessing that he did not know how to read, Mr. Temple said, "It is merely a request to a powerful friend to get me a lawyer. Come, man. Do I not deserve a lawyer?"

"See what I can do," said the soldier. "But I can't read. What's the name of the gentleman I've to take this to?"

Mr. Temple told him.

The soldier whistled under his breath. "Take it when my duty is over," he said.

Mr. Temple watched him like a hawk until he was relieved of his duty. He waited anxiously, dreading to see the soldier produce that note and show it to the relief guard. But the sentry walked away whistling. Now all Mr. Temple had to do was wait. They had promised to help him if he were ever in any trouble. He had told of Mrs. Carruthers's betrayal in his note. It was up to them to deal with her. Had it not been for her, he would still be at liberty.

All that night he waited. When would *his* sentry come on duty again? The next day with a stoicism that amazed his interrogators, he continued to protest his innocence.

At last when they were gone, he rushed to the bars, and there was the sentry parading up and down. He called him over. "What news?"

"He says as how you're to confess to the murder of Carruthers and deny being a traitor. That way, they'll move you to Newgate instead o' the Tower, and he can get you out of there."

"You are sure?"

"Cross me heart. That's what he says. Sounds daft to me. Here." The sentry fished in a capacious pocket and looked quickly around. "He's sent you some brandy for to keep yer spirits up."

"Later," said Mr. Temple urgently, hearing the key turn in the door of his cell.

His faith in his employers was absolute, and that

is what gave him courage to admit to the murder of Guy Carruthers. But the earl, who he was beginning to hate with a passion, merely smiled at him and said mockingly, "We know you murdered Carruthers, but you shall be kept here without food and water until you give us the names of the other traitors."

Left alone, Mr. Temple sat down wearily. They had failed him. How long could he hold out? He could not go on much longer without food and water. Perhaps he would have been better to have used his four precious guineas to bribe the sentry to bring him a meal. The brandy! That was something. He called to the sentry.

"Dead," said the earl to Annabelle. "Stone dead. Poisoned. A bottle of brandy found its way into his cell, and no one will say how it got there. The sentries are old Waterloo campaigners, and my suggestion that one of them might have passed the bottle through the bars was met with horror. But someone got it to him. However, as I told you, he did confess to the murder of your husband. So be careful and should anyone suspicious approach you, inform me immediately."

She sat pale and still, rigid with shock. Although she had just had her worst fears confirmed, it was still a terrible blow.

"It will be in the newspapers, will it not?" she said.

"No, it is being hushed up. I have finally persuaded them to have the two sentries who were on duty outside his cell followed and watched. We must try to find who sent the brandy to him. The sentries have been investigated. Both are brave men, but even brave men will do strange things for money."

He stood up. "Miss Davenant tells me you have not been out of the house. You may have one of my carriages at your disposal. I suggest you start to take the air."

He bowed and left.

Annabelle felt very alone. She could not confide in Miss Davenant because it was being increasingly borne in on her that Miss Davenant not only did not know of her arrangement with the earl, but would certainly not be a party to it if she knew.

Chapter Seven

EACH DAY, Annabelle steeled herself for a visit from the earl, and each day came and went that long summer without him putting in an appearance. She read in the social columns that he had gone to Brighton. Later she read of his return. He had attended a picnic given by Lady Clairmont. His name was linked with Rosamund Clairmont. It was all very odd.

The house rental was paid regularly as was her generous allowance. She and Miss Davenant took leisurely drives, went to Gunter's for ices, sewed in the evenings, and remained on the fringes of society; Annabelle because she felt she had joined the ranks of the "fashionable impure," Miss Davenant because she considered it would not be suitable for the mourning Mrs. Carruthers to attend any functions until the Little Season.

Annabelle did not know that Cressida had sent a letter to her former London house and, failing to receive a reply, assumed that Annabelle had become too grand a London lady to want to be troubled with her old friend from the vicarage. Matilda, too, had called at the house to find new occupants in residence and no news of where Mrs. Carruthers had gone. She did not know that Annabelle had called on her that day for the simple reason that her husband had not told her.

It was an exceptionally fine summer. Miss Davenant's company was undemanding to say the least. She was now more like a placid sheep than an intense one; her snowy, woolly curls as springy as ever, but her face mild and relaxed. Miss Davenant had achieved the dream of every former poor relation—security. She took her job as companion seriously and agreed to every suggestion Annabelle made, although she found Annabelle's desire to visit musty old buildings such as the Tower of London and the Monument sadly unfashionable.

Annabelle had grown in beauty as calm day followed calm day and all bills were paid promptly and the shadows of death, violence, and murder receded from her mind.

One particularly warm and balmy day, she startled Miss Davenant by saying, "Let us go to Vauxhall this evening."

"Do you think that would be wise? Two ladies, unaccompanied?"

"We shall be perfectly safe. We will take James, the footman, to attend us, hire a box, and have an elegant supper. I have never been to Vauxhall," said Annabelle wistfully. "Mr. Carruthers was always promising to take me, but he always forgot."

"I, too, have never seen Vauxhall," said Miss Davenant, beginning to flutter with excitement. "And, of course, if we take James, we shall have nothing to worry about."

And so the elderly chaperon and the young widow giggled like schoolgirls as the carriage bore them over Westminster Bridge. Vauxhall was a great adventure.

Vauxhall Pleasure Gardens lay on the south side of the city. The name was originally Faux Hall, which was corrupted into Vauxhall. It was popularly believed that the name derived from Guy Fawkes, the gunpowder-plot conspirator, but the true derivation was from Faulk de Brent, a famous Norman soldier of fortune to whom King John gave in marriage, Margaret de Ripariis. To that lady belonged the manor of Lambeth to which Faux Hall was annexed.

The admission charge was four shillings each which, as Miss Davenant paid over her share, said was so extravagant it made her feel like the veriest profligate.

Followed by their footman, the two ladies passed through the turnstile and entered the gardens. Annabelle let out a gasp of surprise, and Miss Davenant stood blinking in the sudden blaze of light.

As her eyes became accustomed to the radiance, Annabelle saw that the principal part of the gardens was a quadrilateral, called the grove, bisected by long colonnades. One of the colonnades on Annabelle's right was at least three hundred feet long and covered by an arched Gothic roof where the groins were marked by lines of lamps shedding a golden light and the pendants by single crimson lights at the intersections. In the middle of the grove was an orchestra playing under a large inverted cockleshell canopy, flooded also in a blaze of light.

Annabelle and Miss Davenant linked arms and moved forward as if in a dream. There was so much to see, it was bewildering. There was the rotunda where an equestrian display was taking place. Then further on, they came across a replica of William Tell's cottage, then a statue of Neptune with his horses shooting jets of water from their nostrils, then onto another theater where the Revers family were delighting a crowd with their juggling and acrobatics, then back to the rotunda, drawn by the sound of the music. The display of horsemanship was over, and now a ballet was in progress, the grace and classical beauty of which was rather spoiled, aesthetically at least, by the performances of the tightrope dancers high above the pit where the ballet was being performed.

They watched the performance to the end, standing at the back of the benches, and then a bell rang in the distance, and there was a great rush of people in the direction of its sound. "The fireworks!" cried a man.

"Fireworks," breathed Annabelle, and almost dragging Miss Davenant after her, she followed the crowd.

The fireworks had been made by that magician, D'Ernst. Annabelle gazed up open-mouthed at the concentric circles of gold and silver and blue and red. Snakes of red fire twisted across the sky, rockets rushed up toward the moon and cascaded down in golden tears, silver stars, and amber balls.

Annabelle, dazed and happy, clutched hold of Miss Davenant and laughed with delight. During the last portion of the fireworks display, which featured a gorgon's head with snaky red tresses and flaming eyeballs, a child of some nine years could be seen, walking through the fire and glitter on a tightrope.

To Annabelle, who had never really had much

fun in her life, it was the most stupendous thing she had ever seen.

They walked away when the display was over, still too intrigued about the delights of Vauxhall to trouble about finding a supper box. There was so much still to see. At the end of one of the walks was a Gothic arch with an illuminated transparency behind it of broken pillars and a large stone cross. In the darker walks, statuary gleamed whitely among the trees, and always there was the sound of music and the excitement in the air engendered by hundreds of Londoners making the most of the best spectacle the city had to offer.

At last, they began to feel tired and hungry. There were supper boxes lining some of the main walks, but they were all full. They went to the pavilion and stood in the entrance blinking in the light from hundreds of lamps reflected in the mirrored walls.

Annabelle saw the master of ceremonies and with a social courage she did not know she possessed, she approached this grand individual and explained that they were hungry but had not reserved a supper box. He smiled and said one had just been vacated and ushered them into it, a sulky look crossing his face as he realized that Annabelle had not noticed his outstretched palm and had no intention of tipping him.

They ordered ham, rack punch, and salad, talking all the time about the delights they had seen while the stalwart James stood behind their chairs.

In a box on the other side of the room was the earl, paying court to Rosamund Clairmont, accompanied by her parents. Lady Clairmont studied the earl's handsome face and wondered when he was going to propose marriage to her daughter.

The earl, like every other gentleman of the Regency, had been brought up to believe that women were for passion and ladies for marriage. But somehow Rosamund never seemed to excite his senses. What worried him was why he should expect her to. She would make a suitable wife. He was man of the world enough to know now that her sliding glances, which promised a world of sin, were only part of an act. Underneath it all he suspected she was rather cold. She was child enough to enjoy the gaudy pleasures of Vauxhall, a place he had visited too often in his youth to remain enchanted. The chattering noise of conversation rising from the supper boxes around the mirrored room was immense.

"My dear, everything you say intrigues me," he said automatically to the questioning glance cast up at him and the confiding little dimpled hand on his arm. He had not been listening to a word, but knew from experience that Rosamund's conversation was undemanding to say the least, and he only needed to interject some flirtatious remark to keep her happy while he went on with his own thoughts.

After all, he *was* being hard on the chit. His jaded eye traveled around the room. The ladies in the other boxes looked remarkably the same, depending on age-group. The young girls were in white muslin with pomaded hair and small painted mouths. Any female cursed with a largish mouth painted a little rosebud mouth in the middle of it. In all, they had a uniform appearance. The mothers were more rouged and harder of eye, but affected the same *jeune fille* fashions as their daughters, high-waisted gowns with little puff sleeves, gloves to the elbow, long, draped scarves.

And then he saw Annabelle. For a moment he did not recognize her. His gaze was arrested because she was laughing in a happy, carefree way. She was in half mourning, a beautifully cut gown of lilac silk edged with gray. Her thick brown curls shone in the candlelight, and her large eyes sparkled.

Beside her sat his aunt. Miss Davenant was no longer festooned in bits and pieces but attired in a gown of plum-colored corded silk of a Parisian cut. On her woolly white curls was a modish turban. Her happy sheep's face gazed around the room with childlike pleasure. And then she saw the earl. She raised her hand in greeting and said something to Annabelle. Annabelle looked at the earl, and all her joy and delight in the evening were wiped from her face.

"And so," went on Rosamund with a ripple of laughter, "Lady Baxter said, 'Not on my best rug, my dear,' and Lord Baxter replied . . ."

Her voice trailed off. Lady Clairmont looked at the earl sharply. He was sitting, transfixed.

"Excuse me," he said. "I have just seen my aunt. Must pay my respects."

Lady Clairmont raised her quizzing glass and watched as the earl crossed the room. "Pooh!" said her daughter. " 'Tis that pretty Mrs. Carruthers. Thank goodness she is married."

"You have forgot," said Lady Clairmont dryly, "the fire at the Manor. Guy Carruthers died."

"So he did," said Rosamund. "So she's a widow. Mama, what has gone wrong? You yourself said that Darkwood would propose before the end of the Season, but nothing happened, and now the Little

Season will soon be upon us bringing more debutantes to London."

"Peace, my child. We are of the aristocracy, and Mrs. Carruthers is only of the gentry. Darkwood knows what he owes to his name. Whenever did an aristocrat marry for love!"

Rosamund pouted. It was very lowering to think that a man might marry one for one's rank, although infinitely preferring the charms of someone else.

The earl bent over Annabelle's hand. "You must excuse my neglect, Mrs. Carruthers," he said. "I have been very busy."

"Yes, we can see *that*," said his aunt gaily. "Such a pretty young lady. Who is she?"

"Miss Rosamund Clairmont," he replied.

"Very suitable," said Miss Davenant with satisfaction. "A good name and a good dowry."

"Are you happy?" the earl asked Annabelle abruptly.

The truthful answer to that was, Yes, very, up until the moment I saw you.

But Annabelle confined herself to a "Yes, I thank you, my lord."

"We have been having such fun," burbled Miss Davenant. "Do you not think I am become modish, Darkwood? Mrs. Carruthers plies a magic needle."

"Vastly fetching," said the earl. He saw the shadows of worry and shame fleeting across Annabelle's eyes and realized she still considered herself his mistress. He must disabuse her, but Vauxhall was not the place.

"I shall call on you tomorrow afternoon," he said. "We have a certain ... er ... business matter to discuss."

"Will three o'clock be suitable?" asked Annabelle.

"Very suitable."

He bowed and left.

"He will find all the accounts in order," said Miss Davenant with satisfaction. "And although he has been very generous, he will find we have not taken advantage of his generosity."

Annabelle sat with her eyes lowered, trying to disguise the feeling of shock mixed with shame that coursed through her body. She had been living for the minute, almost forgetting her disgraceful arrangement with the earl. She wanted to leave, but there was a further shock to come.

"Look at that elegant couple," cried Miss Davenant.

Annabelle raised her eyes and then sat rigid. Matilda and her husband, the duke, were promenading along the front of the boxes, stopping here and there to speak to friends. Matilda was wearing a gown of apple green silk embroidered with gold corn sheaves. There was a heavy tiara of diamonds on her golden hair and a collar of magnificent diamonds about her neck. The duke cut a fine figure in black evening dress with white cravat and white silk stockings embroidered with gold clocks. There was a large diamond in his cravat and diamond buckles on his shoes. Only his wife and his valet knew that the breadth of his shoulders and chest and apparent strength of his calves were due to clever buckram wadding rather than muscle.

Matilda saw Annabelle and exclaimed, "Why there is Annabelle, Mrs. Carruthers!"

A man in one of the supper boxes near her started in surprise and then raised his quizzing glass.

"Walk on," commanded the duke icily. "You know I do not approve of such a friendship."

Matilda turned pink with anger, but she smiled at Annabelle as they passed and rolled up her eyes in comical dismay toward her stony-faced husband.

"What odd behavior," said Miss Davenant.

"That was Matilda, Duchess of Hadshire and her husband," said Annabelle. "We were once friends, but her husband does not approve of the friendship."

"Then he must be a very odd man," said Miss Davenant, taking a hearty swig of rack punch. "You are all that is respectable, my dear Mrs. Carruthers. He must have rats in his attic."

Despite her distress, Annabelle giggled. "No, he is not mad. Do not drink any more. I fear you are a trifle foxed."

"Not I," said Miss Davenant. "A little to go, that is all."

Annabelle did not want to spoil her companion's evening and so continued to drink punch, which tasted of licorice, and eat ham, which now tasted like cardboard.

With relief, she saw that Miss Davenant was finally becoming sleepy and was able to urge her to leave.

Two hours before the earl was due to arrive the next day, Matilda appeared and threw herself into Annabelle's arms. "I had the deuce of a time finding where you lived," said Matilda. "Why did you not tell me? How long have you been here?"

Annabelle turned to Miss Davenant and said, "Please leave us for a little, if you do not mind. We have something private to discuss."

Miss Davenant obediently put her knitting back in her workbag. But once outside the door, she hesitated, and then leaned an ear against the panels to listen. Mrs. Carruthers had been looking frightened and worried, but would not say what was troubling her. Perhaps she would tell the duchess. Miss Davenant felt it her duty to listen. How could she help poor Mrs. Carruthers if she did not know what ailed her?

"Sit down, Matilda," she heard Annabelle say quietly. "You should not be here."

"Hadshire does not know," said Matilda airily. "I told him I was making calls. The carriage servants do not know who lives here, so they cannot tell him. But what has been happening to you? I heard about the fire and about Guy's death. Thank goodness he has obviously left you enough to live comfortably."

"He left me nothing," said Annabelle. "I do not know why you are here, Matilda. I called on you after I had been thrown out of our town house and had nowhere to go. I was desperate. But your butler told me you wanted to have nothing to do with me."

"Annabelle, Annabelle, all the servants are the duke's creatures. The butler would go straight to him, not to me. He must have enjoyed sending that message on my behalf. But tell me all. How do you come to be living with Darkwood's aunt? Yes, I know who she is, for I asked everyone until I found out."

Annabelle told her first about Guy's death being murder, about how he had gambled the Manor away, and about how he had been working for traitors who had killed him.

"Quite like a Gothic novel," exclaimed Matilda

in horror. "How frightened and miserable you must have been. But how come you here?"

Miss Davenant pressed her ear harder against the door.

"I am Darkwood's mistress."

Behind the door, Miss Davenant blinked.

"Never!" cried Matilda. "You cannot be. My dear innocent, one does not foist one's mistress off on one's aunt!"

"It is all very odd," sighed Annabelle. "I had nowhere else to go, nothing else to do. He had been kind after the death of Guy, had given me his card. I could not take charity, I had to offer something in return. And I only had myself to offer."

"But could you not have found some sort of employ?" demanded Matilda. "A governess, or something? Surely anything would have been better than to volunteer to join the ranks of the ladies of cracked reputation."

"It is easy to be wise now," said Annabelle. "You must realize I was desperate."

"And when did your amorous relations with the wicked earl begin?"

"They haven't. I mean, it is most strange. He placed me here with Miss Davenant as chaperon, but he has not come near me since. I saw him at Vauxhall before I saw you. He is coming to call this afternoon."

"And his aunt who looks all that is respectable countenances this relationship?"

"She does not know."

"She . . ." Matilda opened her mouth to lecture Annabelle further and then suddenly closed it again. There was something very odd here. Not a whisper had she heard of Darkwood having Annabelle as mistress, and Matilda heard all the whispers.

"Begin at the beginning again," said Matilda quietly, "and tell me all."

A hand to her cushionlike bosom, Miss Davenant listened outside the door as intently as Matilda did in the drawing room inside.

"And you really must go, Matilda," said Annabelle finally. "It is not proper for you to be visiting such as I."

"Pooh! Surely our friendship can survive an illicit affair?" said Matilda in her forthright way. "You shall hear from me further. Do you know Emma will be back in London soon?"

"Do not tell her," said Annabelle in a low voice. "She is not as strong-minded as you and would be deeply distressed."

"But she will want to see you! Never mind. It is all very odd."

Miss Davenant waddled quickly up the narrow stairs to her bedchamber and sat down, her legs shaking.

Why on earth was Darkwood about to behave in such a manner? To put his own aunt in charge of his doxy?

But Mrs. Carruthers was not a doxy. She was a gentle, caring lady. The liaison with the earl had not yet begun.

Miss Davenant saw her duty clearly and felt a sense of relief. This affair should never begin, and she herself would see to it. The earl had made her an allowance for life. Well, she and Annabelle could live together quietly on that. She had not very great courage, but the first time the earl showed signs of staying the night, then that was the time that Miss

Davenant would confront him. She was used to her rich relatives treating her with contempt. Darkwood obviously thought she would do anything for money. In the meantime she meant to enjoy her new financial freedom as much as possible and, having put all thoughts of action off to some misty future, Miss Davenant made her way downstairs again to join Annabelle.

Meanwhile, outside, Matilda dismissed her carriage and servants, saying she wanted to walk for a little and took a hack straight to the earl's town house where she demanded an audience with him. As a married woman and a duchess, she knew she could risk doing so without fear of disgrace, except in the eyes of her husband.

Bursting with curiosity, Barnstable announced her, not noticing in his interest in this beautiful duchess's unconventional call that his master's eyes were glittering feverishly.

The earl glared at the dainty duchess. His head felt hot and heavy. That damned fever was returning.

"State your business, Your Grace," he said sharply.

"I am come to demand to know your intentions regarding Mrs. Carruthers."

"None of your business."

"Fustian. A friend of mine, a gently bred lady coolly informs me that she has arranged to become your mistress. You not only accepted her, but put your poor aunt in residence as chaperon. It will be the talk of London. Not only will Annabelle's reputation be ruined, but that of your aunt. Have you no shame?"

The earl was not the first man to be startled by

the rather deep and commanding voice issuing from such a pretty and dainty face.

He felt the fever tightening its grip. Angry as he was, all he wanted to do was to get rid of her.

"My dear duchess," he said icily, "if you are a friend of hers, then you should have helped her in her hour of need. As it stands, she came to me with her silly offer. I have no intention of making Annabelle Carruthers my mistress. I shall call on her shortly and tell her so. She may remain my pensioner until she marries again."

"Oh," said Matilda, nonplussed. "Why did you not tell her before?"

"I had other things to concern me and had almost forgot the woman." And yet that was not quite true, he thought foggily. He had never forgotten that kiss. He was stubbornly determined to make a good marriage and without ever admitting it to himself, he felt deep down that Annabelle would sway him from his purpose.

Matilda looked at him crossly. She decided he was drunk. "I shall tell her myself," she said firmly.

When she had left, the earl summoned Barnstable. "This damned fever again," he said thickly. "Get me to bed, and tell anyone who asks that I am gone to my estates. I do not want to broadcast my continued weakness around the ton."

Matilda returned home to find the duke waiting for her with his shadow, the brutal Rougement, in attendance.

"You have some explaining to do," said the duke. Matilda could see that he was in an icy rage, and her heart sank. "My servants followed you. After leaving a house in Clarence Square, you took a hack to the Earl of Darkwood's town house and entered without either maid or footman to accompany you. Are you cuckolding me?"

"No, never," said Matilda. "Annabelle Carruthers is being cared for by the earl's aunt. She . . . she was unwell, the aunt, I mean, and Annabelle asked me to convey a message to Darkwood about his aunt's indisposition."

"What a bad liar you make, my love," said the duke. "Rougement here will escort you to your apartments, and there you will stay confined until you choose to tell me the truth. Besides, I forbade you to have anything to do with Mrs. Carruthers."

"I *did* tell you the truth," cried Matilda, determined to lie and lie rather than reveal Annabelle's true situation.

The duke smiled maliciously. "Escort Her Grace, Rougement," he ordered, "and tell the servants that she is to be supplied with nothing but bread and water until she comes to her senses."

Matilda backed away as Rougement approached her, a leer on his face. She was all at once sure he meant to take her by the arm, and she could not bear to be touched by him. She gave a stifled sob and turned and ran up the stairs with Rougement following behind.

Meanwhile Annabelle and Miss Davenant waited and waited for the earl to arrive. At last Annabelle sent a servant to inquire whether he meant to visit her or not. The servant returned with the news that the earl had left for his estates.

Relief mixed with a strange disappointment flooded Annabelle.

"So now we can be comfortable again," said Miss Davenant, "for I must confide that I never liked Darkwood above half!"

While the earl lay in the black grip of his fever, Annabelle and Miss Davenant resumed the gentle pattern of their days. They were driving in the park at the fashionable hour one afternoon when a light carriage drew alongside them, and Annabelle found herself looking into the startled features of Cressida Knight, who was sitting with her aunt, Lady Kitson.

After the introductions had been made, Cressida said, "Do give me your direction, Annabelle, so that I may call."

Annabelle felt miserable. She did not want to risk damaging Cressida's reputation, and it would most certainly be damaged when the news got out that she was visiting a lady of ill repute. If only the earl would do one thing or the other, either take her as mistress or cast her off.

"I am only visiting Miss Davenant at the moment," said Annabelle, "and I would prefer to leave it for a little."

"Oh, *I* see," said Cressida huffily, thinking Annabelle had become too grand to want to know her.

"No, it's not what you think," said Annabelle quickly. "Only that I am not in a position to meet guests. I shall see you very soon."

Cressida gave her a relieved smile. "It is all so strange here," she whispered. "And the gentlemen are so very terrifying."

Lady Kitson bowed to Annabelle and Miss Davenant, Cressida waved cheerfully, and their carriage moved off.

"Now what?" said Annabelle. "Shall we return home?"

"Yes, but there is a fine-looking gentleman staring at you," whispered Miss Davenant. "See, he is stopping."

Annabelle looked across into the square handsome features of a fashionably dressed gentleman who was driving a phaeton with a diminutive tiger perched behind.

He promptly called to his tiger to hold the horses and jumped down and bowed low before Annabelle, sweeping off his hat to reveal a thick head of golden curls.

"Westbourne, at your service, ma'am," he said. "Peter Westbourne. Friend of your late husband. I saw you at Vauxhall but did not consider the place right to offer you my deepest condolences. I often played cards with Carruthers."

"Thank you," said Annabelle, liking his fair hair and blue eyes. "You are most kind. In fact you are the first of my husband's friends to approach me, although I have recognized many of them while driving in the park."

"He was a sad loss," said Mr. Westbourne mournfully. "But you go on well?"

"Yes, I thank you."

"It would give me great pleasure to call on you. May I have your direction?"

Annabelle bit her lip, but Miss Davenant said eagerly, "Number ten, Clarence Square. We are at home most afternoons."

"Then I shall make it my pleasure to call on you very soon."

He bowed again and leapt lightly into his carriage and drove off, his tiger scrambling onto the back strap.

"Now, then," said Miss Davenant, pleased. "*That*

is a pretty fellow. Westbourne . . . let me see. I must find out about him."

"Some of my husband's friends were not all that is respectable," said Annabelle. "And we do not know anything about this Mr. Westbourne at present."

"But I shall find out," said Miss Davenant. "Oh, yes, I shall find out."

To that end Miss Davenant departed the following afternoon to call on various ladies of the impoverished aristocracy with whom she had remained on close terms.

While she was gone, Annabelle received a call from Mr. Westbourne.

As she was a widow, there was nothing unconventional about her receiving a visit alone from a young man. Mr. Westbourne, she felt, was an antidote to the earl. He was unaffected and sunny-natured and above all, he seemed to admire her greatly. He only stayed the regulation ten minutes, but got her to promise to go driving with him on the following day.

Her heart lifted when Miss Davenant returned, bubbling over with good news.

"It seems Mr. Westbourne hails from the Sussex Westbournes; father is a retired admiral, mother was a Jacey from Kent, distantly related to the Earl of Exminster's family, comfortable income, unmarried, what could be better?"

"I do not think I want to marry again, if that is what you mean," said Annabelle.

"But you must!" exclaimed Miss Davenant. "It is the only way out of . . ." She colored with embarrassment.

Annabelle looked at her curiously. "What were you about to say, Miss Davenant?"

Miss Davenant looked miserable.

"I think you know," said Annabelle gently.

Miss Davenant hung her head.

"I take your silence to be an affirmative answer. Miss Davenant, I shall take a risk. I believe you know I am Darkwood's mistress, and yet I cannot understand how you allowed yourself to be used in this way."

"But I didn't know, not until I overheard you telling the Duchess of Hadshire. I should not have listened, but I was concerned for you. I thought that when Darkwood finally decided to take you up on your offer, I would suggest we find somewhere cheap and pleasant, like a little cottage, and you could live with me, for Darkwood has made me an allowance for life. But you should marry again, and when I saw Mr. Westbourne, so fine and fair, I could not help hoping . . ."

Annabelle's eyes misted with tears. "You are so very kind, and you make me feel so spineless. I must have been mad to ever offer myself to Darkwood. I had a little money. I could have taken cheap lodgings and tried to find work as a governess."

Miss Davenant held up her hands in horror. "A lifetime of respectable and impoverished gentility, being bullied by pupils and abused by their masters! Heaven forbid."

"There is so little women can do to turn an honest penny," said Annabelle, half to herself. "All the jobs are done by men—even the mantua makers are men and the staymakers."

"God put us in our appointed stations in society,"

said Miss Davenant firmly, "and to try to lower oneself is flying in the face of divine providence."

"I often worry about that," said Annabelle with her chin on her fist. "It is a wonderful belief for we need not feel guilty about the poor and they need not envy the aristocracy, but if all men are born equal, then why are we supposed to accept such an idea?"

"Fie, for shame!" said Miss Davenant robustly. "You must not pity the poor, for they do not have the same feelings as we and not being nearly so refined, they do not have our sensibilities."

"I wonder," mused Annabelle. "When a lady loses, say, her father, she weeps and moans and is cosseted by her friends and treated by the physician. When the father of a servant dies, she is allowed one day off, if she is lucky, to attend the funeral and then is expected to get back to work and if she cries too much, she may be dismissed. I have even heard my late husband complain about a weeping maid, saying she was too depressing and did not know her place, and how dare she affect the sensibilities of her betters. You yourself must have been in straitened circumstances to take such a post."

"Yes," agreed Miss Davenant, "but that is different. My circumstances were *genteely* straitened."

Annabelle began to laugh. "What a fix I am in and how relieved I am that you know. If you could bear to have me as a pensioner for a little, Miss Davenant, I could set up as a dressmaker."

"But the long hours! The drudgery!"

"Only for a little if I am successful. Then I can soon hire seamstresses."

"It is every young lady's duty to marry," admonished Miss Davenant. "But if we aim to be independent ladies, I think we should tell my nephew as soon as possible."

"If he ever returns from the country," said Annabelle.

The next day, while Annabelle enjoyed a drive in the park with Mr. Westbourne, the earl recovered from his fever and felt very sorry for himself. No one had called. He had forgotten his instructions to Barnstable to tell everyone he was out of town. His bed felt uncomfortable, and although his bedroom was still clean, there were no fresh flowers, and there was no cool hand on his forehead and no quiet voice to read to him.

He felt irrationally angry with Annabelle. He did not expect her to be his mistress, but he felt he did merit a little sympathetic attention from that quarter.

And then on the following day as he sat in the library wrapped in a dressing gown, still feeling weak, he received a surprise visit. Barnstable, considering him fit to receive visitors ushered in the vicar and his daughter, Cressida.

They fussed around him and quite restored him to a good temper with their obvious concern for his health.

"I met Mrs. Carruthers in the park the other day," said Cressida. "She was driving with a Miss Davenant."

"Yes, my aunt. She is staying with her."

"How odd! Annabelle, Mrs. Carruthers, would not give me her address. I wonder why?"

The earl cursed inwardly. He must see Mrs. Carruthers as soon as possible and tell her she was simply his pensioner, nothing more. Of course, she would shy away from having respectable visitors. It was this damned fever which kept addling his wits.

After Mr. Knight and Cressida had left, the earl called for his valet and asked for his carriage to be brought around. He must see Mrs. Carruthers without any further delay.

Chapter Eight

*M*ISS DAVENANT JUMPED in surprise as the earl was announced. Annabelle was out driving in the park with Mr. Westbourne.

"Sit down, nephew," she said faintly. "Mrs. Carruthers is out taking the air with a . . . with a friend. Have you just returned?"

"I have not returned from anywhere," said the earl crossly. "I have been ill, extremely ill."

Miss Davenant reflected cynically that men were always "extremely" ill. "But your butler told our footman that you had gone to your estates."

The earl's face cleared. "I wondered why no one came around to bathe the fevered brow. Now that I remember, I did say to Barnstable to say that I was away from home. I suddenly did not want the ton to know of my illness. Pride, I suppose."

He gave his aunt a blinding smile. Miss Davenant blinked. He was too disgracefully handsome. Annabelle must not be put at risk.

"It is pleasant here," said the earl stretching out his booted legs. He looked about him. The drawing room was filled with vases of flowers. The windows were open to the square where the russet-colored leaves of autumn fluttered to the ground. There was dainty furniture in the drawing room upholstered in yellow silk with heavy gold brocade curtains at the windows. A little gilt clock ticked busily over the mantel, and a small fire crackled on the hearth sending out a pleasing smell of woodsmoke.

"Yes, we are very happy," sighed Miss Davenant. "I shall be sorry to leave."

"How so? Is Mrs. Carruthers thinking of marrying again so soon?"

"Now, how could she, when she is tied to you by that terrible promise." Miss Davenant blushed deep red and stared miserably at the earl.

"So she told you. Well, I am here to tell her I never at any time wanted her as mistress. I had a feeling she might not take charity. My dear aunt, do you think for a moment I would have placed you in residence with a doxy?"

"I do not really know," said Miss Davenant pathetically. "And men can be so very wicked. Mrs. Carruthers is so beautiful. I thought you were going to snatch her like a blossom and then cast her off like a worn-out glove."

"My dear aunt!"

"Well, that is what they are always doing in the books I read. They are always casting off ladies like worn-out gloves."

"I have no intention of casting either of you off. I will continue to make you an allowance for life, Aunt, as I should have done this long time past. As for Mrs. Carruthers, her allowance will continue plus a dowry, and I sincerely hope that she will soon find a husband to take care of her financially as soon as a decent period of mourning has been observed."

"Oh, you are so good!" exclaimed Miss Davenant.

"She will not have to start that dreadful dressmaking business, and I will not have to protect her honor, for I was prepared to do mortal battle with you, Darkwood, if you so much as laid a finger on her."

"Do not become so exercised," said the earl lazily, "I have plans to lay all of my fingers on someone else, and with respectable intentions."

"Was it that dark little frumpy creature I saw you with at Vauxhall?"

"That dark little frumpy creature as you very well know is accounted the most notable beauty in London. She is Rosamund Clairmont as I already told you, and I intend to make her my bride."

"Are you so very much in love with her?"

"I respect her. She would make a most suitable wife and hostess."

"How dull!"

There came a rattle of carriage wheels from outside. "That will be Annabelle," cried Miss Davenant, running to the window. The earl rose in a leisurely way and joined her. The long windows opened onto a little wrought-iron balcony. The earl leaned over.

Annabelle Carruthers was being helped down from a phaeton by a handsome young man. She was wearing one of the new "transparent" hats, a creation of stiffened gauze. She stood for a moment talking to the gentleman who then kissed her hand.

The earl felt a tide of anger well up in him. Here was a woman who believed herself to be his mistress, and yet she was cavorting about London like the veriest lightskirt. He had a damned good mind not to tell her the true circumstances of the arrangement, but as soon as Annabelle had entered the room, Miss Davenant flew at her, burbling out the good news.

Annabelle looked past her to where the earl was coming in from the balcony. He looked remote and severe. She dropped him a curtsy and thanked him warmly but then alarmed Miss Davenant by saying she could not live on his charity for much longer and that she planned to become a dressmaker.

She unpinned her hat as she spoke. She was wearing a gown of lilac silk trimmed with black ribbons and with a mantle of gray silk over it. Her rich brown hair shone with little fiery lights, and she exuded that tantalizing air of fragility and femininity that Rosamund tried so hard to achieve without success. He looked at her mouth and remembered that kiss at the inn. Miss Davenant stood between them, her mouth slightly open, looking from one to the other in dawning surprise. She always said afterward that the very air of the room had become charged with intense emotion and electricity, like the air just before a thunderstorm or a shock from one of Dr. Galvan's machines.

Then the earl said abruptly, "As you will. But do not involve my aunt in your dressmaking scheme. It is beneath her dignity."

"Oh, no," wailed Miss Davenant. "We could take a sweet little cottage in, say, Hampstead, honeysuckle, and lambs and shepherds and live very quietly, and all the grand ladies would come to order gowns from Mrs. Carruthers."

"Grand ladies are not going to travel to Hampstead or anywhere else," said the earl testily. "They expect the dressmaker to come to them."

Annabelle smiled. "It is not such a mad scheme as it sounds, my lord, and I am sure I would soon be able to repay your generosity. I would certainly live somewhere closer to the center of London than Hampstead."

The earl decided to play for time. He most certainly did not want to see his aunt involved in trade. "Perhaps it would be better if we discussed this after the Little Season," he said. "Your friends, the Knights, are in town, and Miss Knight would be glad of your company."

"Very well," said Annabelle reluctantly. She would have to find time and tranquility to digest all he had just told her. He did not want her as mistress. That news which should have delighted her left her feeling oddly flat.

"Who is the gentleman with whom you were driving?" demanded the earl.

"A Mr. Peter Westbourne."

"Of the Sussex Westbournes," said Miss Davenant eagerly, "for you may be sure I found out all about him. Old Mrs. Harris, you remember, the lady who is fourth cousin of Lord Honeyford, told me she remembers Peter Westbourne as a boy. He must be twenty-eight now, and unmarried."

"I have never heard of the Sussex Westbournes. Which part of Sussex?"

"Let me think. Oh, I have it. Brighton. A little outside, Wedderston, the Westbournes of Wedderston, that's it."

"He has taken a box at the playhouse, Miss Davenant," said Annabelle, "and we are both invited this evening to see *Love's Revenge* or *The Wicked Count Vanquished*."

Miss Davenant clapped her hands in delight.

"May I point out, Mrs. Carruthers," said the earl,

feeling bad-tempered and middle-aged, "that you are still in mourning."

"Mr. Westbourne thought of that," said Annabelle. "I shall be seated in the back of the box, and we shall leave before the harlequinade. All very proper," she added, sensing she was irritating the earl by her friendship with Mr. Westbourne and finding she was enjoying doing so. Before the earl could say anything further, Annabelle went on, "I believe I shall soon have the pleasure of congratulating you on your engagement."

"Yes," he said stiffly. He tried to conjure up Rosamund's face, but found he could not.

"Do you remember Mr. Temple?" he asked.

"How could I forget?" said Annabelle.

"Then may I counsel you to be careful of any man who suddenly shows an interest in you."

Annabelle's eyes flashed with amusement. "My lord, it may amaze you to know that some gentlemen actually do admire me for myself alone and do not have any plots in mind to harm me or strangle me."

"You are well enough in your way," he said, studying her. "It is a pity about your mouth."

"What is up with my mouth?"

"Well, it *is* a trifle large."

"Nephew, I beg of you!" cried Miss Davenant, appalled at such rudeness.

"But I, unlike you, am still young," said Annabelle sweetly, "and do not have one white hair in my head."

"Neither have I," snapped the earl.

Annabelle moved toward him. Her hand darted up and tweaked one solitary white hair out of the shining black. "See!" she said triumphantly. "But

I should not tease you about your age. I am sure when I become as old as you, I shall be touchy about the subject as well."

"You jade!" he said laughing. "There, I am still tetchy from the fever, and you must forgive my rudeness." He smiled down into her eyes and raised her hand, which trembled in his to his lips. Then he stood, still holding her hand, looking at her, while a strong current of feeling seemed to flow from one to the other and back again.

"Do come and look at the leaves," said Miss Davenant from the window, feeling she must distract them or they would fall to insulting each other again. "So brown and gold, but not red, like in the country. Why is that, do you think?"

"Either the soil or the species of tree," said the earl absently. "Plane trees do not have red leaves in the autumn."

"You are holding my hand so tightly, you are hurting it," said Annabelle breathlessly.

He dropped her hand and said in a husky voice, "I shall call again soon. Just to see how you go on."

"Well!" gasped Miss Davenant when he had left. "I thought you might be going to strike each other."

"Infuriating man," said Annabelle Carruthers.

She tried to forget about the earl that evening and enjoy the sunny and undemanding company of Mr. Westbourne, but somehow the earl's words about Mr. Temple returned to her, and she studied her masculine companion when he was absorbed in the play.

She noticed that he wore paint, not all that unusual, but odd in so young a man. And then, around his eyes was a fine network of tiny wrinkles. Perhaps he had spent some time in the Peninsula Wars under a hot sun. Then she blamed the earl for having made her overcritical. But she should have shown him more gratitude. What had come across her that she had been so pert and saucy? He had said he would call again, and then she would be all that was meek and modest and proper. Suddenly the full relief of what he had said flooded over her at last. She was still respectable. She would be able to see Matilda and Emma when she arrived. She would be able to entertain Cressida and perhaps go to a few balls and parties, and then by the end of the Little Season, she could put it about discreetly that she was about to go into business.

Perhaps she could even make gowns for Rosamund. But Rosamund! Surely the earl deserved better, thought Annabelle, who a bare half hour before would have told anyone who asked that the earl and Miss Clairmont were well suited. Her thoughts turned this way and that but always came back to that afternoon with the Earl of Darkwood. He had held her hand so tightly. Had he felt that strange current of emotion? Or was he such a practiced rake that he excited any woman he turned his attention on?

She wondered if he thought of her, and then immediately reminded herself that a rich and handsome earl was so feted and petted by the female sex that he probably had put her out of his mind in the same way that he had done so successfully during the long months of summer.

A week passed, and the earl did not call. Annabelle settled down to enjoy her new friendship with Mr. Westbourne. He never said anything very clever or wise, but he was always amiable and very, very flattering. And then one day as they walked in the park, Annabelle having teasingly said that if she did not get any exercise she soon would become fat, he startled her by asking rather abruptly if she were satisfied that her husband's death had been due to an accident.

She looked up into his guileless blue eyes and said after a little hesitation, "As a matter of fact, Mr. Westbourne, it was not. I cannot explain the circumstances, because they are by way of being a military secret, so do not question me further."

"There are many things about you that disturb me," he said, swiping at a bush with his short stick. "You are not related to Darkwood, I believe."

"No, but he is most kind. The Manor, where I lived with my husband, was next to Delaney, the earl's home. Darkwood likes to help all those in trouble in the village of Upper Chipping. He also owns the land on which the village is built. He kindly arranged for me to take a house with his aunt as chaperon."

"But it is rumored that he plans to marry Rosamund Clairmont!"

"So I believe."

"And so your husband was killed you say? And was the villain brought to justice?"

"Not by the law. He drank poisoned brandy sent to him by one of his colleagues. Now, you must not ask me any more."

The earl walked slowly through the churchyard of St. James in Wedderston, near Brighton. He was looking for a certain grave. Where had the vicar said it was? Ah, yes, over by the south wall. A chill wind was blowing in from the sea, and red and gold leaves fluttered in front of him over the sheep-cropped grass.

And then he saw it. A tall tombstone stood nearly against the wall. The inscription had been chiseled deep and he could read it easily: "PETER THADIUS JOHN WESTBOURNE, BELOVED SON OF THE LATE JOHN PEREGRINE WESTBOURNE, ESQ. AND HIS WIFE, AMELIA. BORN 1792–DIED 1805. HE SLEEPS IN ABRAHAM'S BOSOM."

So it was true. Peter Westbourne had been a boy of thirteen when he had died of cholera. The widowed Mrs. Westbourne had gone to live in Italy, but a woman who had worked as housemaid for the Westbournes had told the earl of the death of the boy. There was no other Peter Westbourne.

He wheeled about and hurried through the cemetery.

Annabelle was in danger.

Of course, London was full of adventurers under assumed names, but after the death of Temple, it was too much of a coincidence that Westbourne, or whoever he was, should appear on the scene.

Annabelle was taking tea with Cressida. She had sent a note around to Lady Kitson's begging Cressida to call. The ladies were alone, Miss Davenant having gone to lie down, saying she felt fatigued after such late nights as they had been keeping.

Cressida thought it was all so romantic that Annabelle should be living with the earl's aunt. She listened with half-concealed delight as Annabelle told her of being turned out of the town house because Guy had given the deeds to a moneylender and of her having to appeal to the earl. The fact that Annabelle might have suffered dreadfully through these adventures did not strike Cressida, who still looked on life as an extension of the plays constantly acted out in her imagination. But Annabelle did not know this. It was all so comfortable, chatting with Cressida, bringing back fond memories of their times together in the vicarage when they were sewing dresses for that ball.

"It was most kind of him was it not?" breathed Cressida. " 'Tis said he has fixed his attention on Rosamund Clairmont, but to my way of thinking, it is a certain Mrs. Carruthers who has taken his eye."

"No, I assure you," said Annabelle with a laugh. "In any case, it appears our rake has a heart of gold."

"And such a handsome and powerful man," said Cressida. "I do not know what all this talk is about, you know, about him being poorly, for no one has seen any sign of ill health in him."

"Except I," said Annabelle, forgetting to be discreet. "I arrived on his doorstep to ask for help just as he was stricken of the fever and had to nurse him through it."

"In his house!" Cressida's pale eyes were opened to their fullest.

Annabelle blushed. "I should never have told you. You must not tell a soul, Cressida, or I should be ruined if it got out."

"No, no," gasped Cressida. "But his aunt was with you?"

"I am afraid not."

"How truly exciting! How very, very romantic! Did you bathe his fevered brow?"

"Yes, Cressida, but it was not at all romantic,

you must realize, and quite shameful of me to have been there at all. I was in such distress when I was thrown out of my home, I did not know what to do. It was a silly and dangerous move. But, oh, I have such fear of the workhouse, for you must understand that Guy left me with nothing at all."

"Pale and destitute, standing weeping on his doorstep," said Cressida half to herself.

Annabelle looked at her in sharp alarm. She had always known Cressida to be a rather scholarly yet sensible girl, for Cressida did not often betray the immature and romantic side of her nature.

Annabelle leaned forward. "I beg you, Cressida, do not breathe a word of this."

"Have I not just given you my word?" said Cressida huffily.

Annabelle bit her lip. Why on earth had she betrayed herself to Cressida? But before she could ask for further assurances of secrecy, Matilda, Duchess of Hadshire was announced.

Cressida remembered she had promised to read to Lady Kitson and reluctantly left.

"Are you well?" asked Annabelle when they were alone. "You look ill!"

"All paint," said Matilda with a laugh. "I shall tell you what happened, for when I last left you I went straight to Darkwood to ask him what he was about."

"Oh, no!" exclaimed Annabelle.

"Oh, yes, and he told me he had only pretended to accept you as his mistress. But when I returned home, those servants of my husband had followed me—I took a hack—and reported that I had gone to Darkwood's town house, and Hadshire had me locked up by that creature of his, Rougement. Nothing but bread and water until I confessed the real reason for my visit. I did not know what to do. I thought out lie after lie for I was mortally tired of bread and water, but nothing would please him. So then I decided to become ill. I painted my face with blanc and put shadows under my eyes with lampblack and let my hair get greasy and lank. Finally Rougement noticed my condition and reported it to Hadshire. So of course he let me out!"

"Why? I do not understand."

"Because I am part of his art collection. It was almost as bad as if he had discovered damp on one of his paintings because it had been hung in the wrong part of the house. He does not love me, but he likes to choose my jewels and gowns and show me off. He does not like my voice, but as long as I speak as little as possible when we are out, then he is pleased with me as part of his collection. He was suitably appalled and commanded me to take the air immediately and eat as much as possible. It is just as well, dear Annabelle, that my looks can be immediately restored by scrubbing off the paint and lampblack, for he would not put up with damaged goods about him for long. How do you go on? I assume Darkwood told you the good news?"

"Yes, but I am resolved not to live for much longer on his charity. I have agreed to remain his pensioner until the end of the Little Season, and then I shall set up as a dressmaker."

"Trade!" said Matilda faintly.

"What would you do? You were the one who said I would have been better off finding employment. I am a very good needlewoman."

"But such drudgery until you can establish yourself! Emma! She will be back soon and will no doubt fund you."

"No," said Annabelle quietly. "I would rather work. I am grateful to Darkwood for this temporary security. It has served to restore my spirits almost to what they were before my unfortunate marriage."

Mr. Westbourne was announced. Matilda looked at him curiously as the introductions were made. As he bent over her hand, she heard a faint creak, and Matilda instantly recognized that creak. Mr. Westbourne wore stays. But he seemed a pleasant and ingenuous fellow and genuinely fond of Annabelle. The shrewd duchess suspected he was much older than he appeared to be and that he owed his figure to stays and his complexion to an artful use of paint, but he was just the sort of man one could be comfortable with, and surely that was what Annabelle needed. Darkwood was out of the question. He was a rake, and in any case, it was well-known he was courting Rosamund Clairmont.

Peter Westbourne was not as sunny-natured as usual as he drove Annabelle to the park the following afternoon. He must find some way of killing her without drawing attention to himself. It was a pity, for he found her rather attractive. But she had betrayed Temple to the authorities, and so she must die. It was part of his code that anyone who betrayed the brotherhood of men who were helping Napoleon must be destroyed as a lesson to others. Once someone had joined their band, there was no escape. Anyone overcome by patriotism or scruples or faintheartedness must be shown what happened to anyone who crossed their path, however innocently. But at the moment, all he could do was keep close to her until he saw an opportunity of killing her that would not incriminate him in any way. He could have told one of his men to do it for him, but he prided himself on handling jobs like these himself. It gave him more power.

Annabelle was too absorbed in her own thoughts to notice his change of manner. She had proudly said she did not like to accept charity, but until she got her dressmaking business going, she would be living on Miss Davenant's charity. Miss Davenant, on the other hand, would be sorely distressed to be left out of things. And so the thoughts went on and on in Annabelle's head. Mr. Westbourne's smart phaeton was moving slowly through Hyde Park.

And then Annabelle saw the earl. He was on horseback, reined in under a stand of trees with several officers mounted beside him. He was scanning the passing carriages.

For some reason the sight of him sent a wave of gladness flooding through Annabelle. "Why there is Darkwood!" she cried.

She pointed with her folded parasol in the earl's direction. Mr. Westbourne looked. He saw the earl scanning the crowd, but then he saw the officers with him, and the way the earl suddenly, on spotting him, pointed and shouted an order. He went white under his paint. He uttered an oath and whipped up his horses.

"What are you doing?" screamed Annabelle as he swerved off the walk and sent the carriage plunging crazily through the trees.

"You knew," he said savagely. "I should have killed you long ago."

"You," said Annabelle. "You are one of *them*!"

She twisted around, hanging onto the guardrail. The earl and his officers were gaining on them, but still Mr. Westbourne continued on his headlong course.

Then the earl was alongside. He stood up in the stirrups and plucked Annabelle from the high-perch phaeton as the officers speeded to the front of the phaeton and brought the carriage horses to a plunging, rearing halt.

Mr. Westbourne was dragged out onto the ground and held down. "Take him to Knightsbridge Barracks," ordered the earl. "I shall join you as soon as I have escorted Mrs. Carruthers home. Quickly! Before a crowd gathers."

Amazingly no one had followed them to this secluded part of the park.

The earl dismounted and lifted Annabelle gently down from the saddle.

"Are you unharmed?" he asked. "He did not hurt you?"

Annabelle dumbly shook her head. He gathered her in his arms and held her close. "He is a traitor," he said. "I do not know who he is, but he is not Peter Westbourne. Peter Westbourne died when he was still a boy." He released her and began to walk with her across the grass, leading his horse and telling her quietly of his journey to Brighton. "I think Westbourne is much older than he tries to appear. He probably comes originally from somewhere near Brighton. We shall soon find out. Let us pray he was the ringleader and you will be in no further danger."

Annabelle walked along beside him, still shaken from the fright she had received. "Why did he pretend to be younger than he was?" she asked.

"Vanity, or a desire to do things thoroughly. The real Peter Westbourne would have been twenty-eight had he lived."

They walked on in silence until Annabelle said, "It is very lowering, you know, to find that one's beau was only courting one with a view to murder."

The earl laughed. "When you are over your shock and things have settled down and you can begin to attend some balls and parties, you will find many beaux. I would see you married again, Mrs. Carruthers."

"I have no wish to be married again," said Annabelle. "Once was enough."

"There are many worthy members of the gentry who would make you a suitable husband. This dressmaking idea is nonsense. It is every woman's role in life to find a husband and bear children."

"Are all rakes so pompous?" asked Annabelle sweetly.

"I was simply thinking about your welfare, madam, but if you prefer to starve in a garret going blind over a needle, then that is your affair. I only ask you not to embroil my aunt in your mad schemes."

They continued walking in angry silence until they reached Clarence Square. Annabelle was suddenly angry with herself instead of him. He had ridden to her rescue, and she had never even thanked him. The earl was feeling pompous and middle-aged. Instead of sneering at her bid for independence, he should be encouraging it, offering her money to start her off, and then she could repay him if she wished. He had only been voicing the thoughts about women he had been brought up with. His remarks to her now echoed in his ears, sounding stuffy and uncaring.

She turned and faced him. "My lord," she said, after taking a deep breath, "I beg you to forgive my burst of temper. I am overwrought. I thank you from the bottom of my heart for having come to my aid."

"And I apologize for being so insensitive to your plight." He raised her hand and kissed it. "I must return to the barracks. If possible, I shall call on you this evening and tell you what we have discovered. But all your cares are over. You may run your life as you please. Should you wish to start in business, do so with my help and then repay me if you must."

Annabelle thanked him warmly and went indoors to amaze and enthrall Miss Davenant with the tale of her latest adventures.

Cressida sat reading to Lady Kitson, a duty she enjoyed because her aunt adored all the latest gothic novels. Mr. Knight had left for the country and turned Cressida over to the care of his sister.

Lady Kitson was a fat, lazy, good-natured woman. Her eyesight was not strong, and she was delighted to find that Cressida was happy to read books aloud for hours at a time. So the days passed gently in making a few calls on useful hostesses and going out to balls and parties, concerts, and operas in the evenings.

Cressida finished the last page, and Lady Kitson sighed with pleasure.

"I am so glad novels are *not* like real life," she said. She rang the bell and summoned her maid and asked for her jewel box.

When the jewel box was placed on a table next to her, Lady Kitson searched in it and found a thin string of very fine small sapphires. "Here you are, my chuck," she said holding the necklace out to Cressida. "They'll look excellent with that pretty gown that friend of yours made for you."

"You are too good," said Cressida.

Lady Kitson dismissed maid and jewel box. "Least I can do," she said. "Never enjoyed so many books in my life. Relieves the tedium of the everyday world."

"Things do happen in the real world that are as fantastic as the happenings in books," said Cressida.

"Pooh! What can you know of gothic adventures, my country mouse?"

Cressida gazed worshipfully at the beautiful gems. She wanted to repay Lady Kitson. "I shall tell you," she said, "if you promise not to breathe a word to a soul."

Lady Kitson looked amused. "I? Of course I would not dream of betraying a confidence."

Cressida went to the door, opened it, and peered around it before returning to her seat. "I had to make sure no one was listening," she said.

Lady Kitson gave an indulgent laugh. "Come along then," she said placing her small fat feet in beaded slippers comfortably on the fender, "tell your tale."

At first it was all intriguing and enjoyable to listen to as far as Lady Kitson was concerned. She heard about the ball and the fire and how the Earl of Darkwood had carried Mrs. Carruthers away from the blaze in his arms.

"Go on," she prompted, "this is better than the play."

A wind had risen outside, the fire was crackling cheerfully on the hearth, and the lamps had not yet been lit. It was a setting made for the telling of secrets.

So Cressida went on, describing how poor Annabelle found that the Manor had been lost in a card game and then how the moneylender had taken her town house away from her. She proceeded to relate how Annabelle had gone to the Earl of Darkwood's town house, unaware that now, as she talked, Lady Kitson's normally good-natured face was becoming hard.

When Cressida had finally finished her tale, Lady Kitson said in stern, measured tones, "You are a country innocent and have been gulled, my child. Annabelle Carruthers has ruined her reputation. No *lady* would be seen dead in an unmarried gentleman's town house. He has set her up with his aunt to provide a thin veneer of respectability over a disgraceful affair. Miss Davenant is a silly woman and would turn a blind eye if asked. You must never go near Annabelle Carruthers again."

"But, Aunt," wailed Cressida, appalled. "You do not know her. She is all that is good and kind."

"I repeat, go near that woman again and I will send you home in disgrace!"

"I have betrayed her," said Cressida, beginning to cry.

Lady Kitson was very fond of her niece. Better to let the girl think the matter had blown over. "There, now, do not cry," she said. "We will say no more about it. I will not breathe a word just so long as you do not visit Clarence Square again."

* * *

The earl called on Annabelle at ten o'clock that evening. He looked tired and strained. He sat down wearily by the fire. "Westbourne's real name was Barry, son of an English cobbler and a French mother. Father died, mother returned to France and became the mistress of one of the tribunal judges during the Terror. The boy was trained from an early age to speak English properly and to act the part of an English gentleman. He was the ringleader of a small group of traitors. They have all been taken. A sentry at Chelsea barracks has disappeared, and we can find no trace of him. It is believed he is the one who conveyed the poisoned brandy to Temple. We want no public fuss about this, we want their masters in France to think they are still working in London. That way, we can watch Barry's apartment and the lodgings of the others and see if anyone sneaks over from France to see how they are doing. They are lucky, for they will not hang. They will be transported to Botany Bay. We are very sure there is no one left to threaten you. You may be comfortable again."

"Thank you," said Annabelle. "Oh, thank you for everything."

He stood up and smiled down at her. "I think I prefer you when you are putting me in my place. Now you must excuse me. I am already late." Something prompted him to say, "I am due to escort Miss Clairmont and her parents to the opera."

It was as if a light had been switched out behind Annabelle's eyes.

He found as he left that he was not looking forward to the evening at all, but stubbornly put down his dismal feelings to fatigue.

Chapter Nine

LADY KITSON WAS TAKING TEA the next afternoon with several society matrons. They were all in the green saloon of Lady Clairmont's home. Balls and gowns were discussed and then the marital hopes of their various daughters and young relatives.

"I think my Cressida will take very well," said Lady Kitson. "She has not much in the way of looks, but she is a sweet and obliging girl."

"Such an expense and worry, this business of puffing them off," sighed Mrs. Camden-Brown, a thin nervous woman who knew her husband would lay the failure at her door if a husband were not found for their equally thin and nervous daughter soon. "Mr. Camden-Brown says that if she is not engaged by Christmas, then he will send us to India, hoping that some young army officer far from home will prove susceptible. But, oh, the long journey, then the heat and the flies."

"I hope it does not happen," replied Lady Kitson. "Things can go so wrong in India. Felicity Hardacre, Lord Hardacre's eldest, was sent there, and what must she do but fall in love with some Indian prince. Of course it would not answer."

"The Hardacres would not countenance her marrying a native?" asked Mrs. Camden-Brown.

"Not in the least. It was the prince's family who did not approve. They considered the girl to be much too inferior."

"My worries will soon be at an end, I think," said Lady Clairmont. "Dear Rosamund could have been wed I do not know how many times over, but she needs must wait for Darkwood to come up to the mark. But he will, my dears, he will."

"I feel sorry for Rosamund should that take place," said Lady Kitson. "One can always turn a blind eye to an opera dancer, say, but to a dashing widow like Mrs. Carruthers, well, that is another matter."

A sudden hush fell on the group, and all eyes turned on Lady Kitson. "What can you mean?" demanded Lady Clairmont icily.

"Lord Darkwood had Mrs. Carruthers in residence in his town house and only shortly after Mr. Carruthers died. Not only that, but he later coerced his own aunt into acting as chaperon to the female."

"Miss Davenant! Never," exclaimed Mrs. Camden-Brown. "I cannot believe it."

"No need to believe me," said Lady Kitson. "I suggest, Lady Clairmont, you tax Darkwood with it yourself. My silly niece, Cressida, found out the whole. I have forbidden her to go near the Carruthers creature. If Mrs. Carruthers cares to ruin herself, that is another matter, but she shall not drag my niece down."

"Impossible," said Lady Clairmont. "Now I suggest we talk of something more interesting."

No one could guess how upset she was as she

talked of balls and parties and operas and poured tea. When her last guest had gone, she rang the bell and asked for a footman to seek out Lord Darkwood and to tell him his presence was urgently required. Rosamund was at the dressmaker's with her maid. Lady Clairmont gave the butler orders that Miss Clairmont was to be told to go to her room and stay there as soon as she arrived back, and if Lord Darkwood was in the house by that time, she was not to be told of it.

After only half an hour, Lord Darkwood arrived and was shown into Lady Clairmont's presence. She looked him over from the top of his shining black hair to the gloss on his Hessian boots and gave a little sigh.

"Sit down, my lord," she said. "I have heard a most curious report.

"There is a niece of Lady Kitson, a certain Cressida Knight."

"Yes, our vicar's daughter."

"Quite. This Cressida is, or was, a friend of a certain Mrs. Carruthers. From Mrs. Carruthers, she gleaned that that lady had been resident in your town house and had nursed you through your fever, that you subsequently set up Mrs. Carruthers in a house in Clarence Square and put your aunt there as well."

"Yes, that is so."

Lady Clairmont took a deep breath. "You have been paying Rosamund a certain amount of attention. I must now tell you that you are no longer welcome in this house and that you are to leave our daughter strictly alone. Do I make myself clear?"

The earl's face darkened. "Is it any use my pointing out that any relations I have with Mrs. Carruthers are perfectly respectable?"

"None whatsoever."

"Then I give you good day," said the earl stonily.

He went straight to Clarence Square, his fury mounting. Annabelle and Miss Davenant were in the drawing room, hemming handkerchiefs.

"Leave us," the earl commanded his aunt. He held open the door for her. "And go straight to your room," he ordered.

Miss Davenant left, feeling frightened and worried. No, she would not go to her room. She would listen. Annabelle might need her help.

"So, madam," said the earl, glaring at Annabelle, "you aimed to marry me all along."

"Marry you? Of course not. Are you foxed?"

"I am cold sober, madam. A very pretty ploy. I try, out of the goodness of my heart, mark you, to save you from scandal, and you—you think by prattling away to Cressida Knight that you can coerce me into marriage. And damn you to hell, you have succeeded."

He sank down into a chair and folded his arms and stared at her moodily.

Annabelle gazed at him in horror. "I told Cressida—I should not—but I told her I had been at your town house. But she swore to me she would not breathe a word to a soul."

"With a secret like that! A young green girl? She talked with the result I have been summoned to Lady Clairmont and ordered to keep clear of her daughter. My aunt's good name is ruined. There is only one thing to do. I shall get a special license, and we will be married as soon as possible."

"Never!" said Annabelle, leaping to her feet. "There is no need."

"Think of my aunt," he said grimly.

Outside the door, Miss Davenant stood, her heart beating hard. She should rush into that room and say she did not care about her name or reputation. But the earl was in love with Annabelle. Of that she was all at once sure. She would gamble. She would simply go to her room as she had been ordered to do and say her prayers and let things take their natural course.

"I *am* thinking of your aunt," said Annabelle. "I shall tell everyone of her innocence."

He rose as well and walked over to face her. "And who would believe you? A doxy like you!"

Annabelle raised her hand to strike him, but he caught it and held it in a firm grip and smiled down at her in a way that made her tremble. "Make the most of it," he said. "You wanted to be my mistress, in any case, so there is no need to shrink from my embrace."

He jerked her into his arms and began to kiss her furiously while she beat at his shoulders helplessly. But gradually she could feel her treacherous body beginning to respond to his embraces, a softening inside, a sweet stab of pain, a yearning, and slowly her hands fell to her side. He bent her back and back until she fell down on the sofa and then he lay on top of her, sinking his mouth further into hers, feeling her body throbbing and pulsating under his own. He forgot he was supposed to be humiliating her and punishing her. He found he could not get enough of her, enough of kisses and caresses. He rolled a little to one side to easier caress her breasts and fell on the floor.

"A pox on these modern sofas," he said. "They were not made for lovemaking."

He stood up and leaned down and drew her to her feet. He kissed her again, warmly and passionately, and then raised his head and flicked one of her tumbled curls with his finger.

"So we are to be married," he said. "Tell my aunt the good news. I will see you again after I have obtained a special license."

He strode downstairs and out of the house. It had been raining earlier, but now the streets were flooded with pale gold sunlight, and the air was fresh and keen. He felt tremendously happy and well.

He thought of Rosamund with her prattling conversation, the seductive exterior, which covered the cold and frosty interior and the cloying scent she wore. "By George!" he said aloud. "I am not going to marry Rosamund Clairmont." And for the first time since he had been a schoolboy, he began to whistle.

Miss Davenant crept into the drawing room. Annabelle was kneeling by the fire, her hair tumbled about her shoulders. She was weeping miserably. "What have I done, Miss Davenant? I have ruined you as well as myself. I told Cressida Knight about staying at Darkwood's town house when he had the fever and what must the silly girl do but spread the story all over town. Now he says he has to m-marry me, and I can't bear it."

Annabelle now meant that she could not bear a loveless marriage to the earl. But as she straightened up and put her tumbled hair back from her face with one shaking hand, Miss Davenant saw a large bruise on her neck. The earl had bitten Annabelle's neck at the height of his passion, but Miss Davenant, innocent herself of any lovemaking experience whatsoever, assumed he had tried to strangle her, and all her dreams of a happy marriage between the earl and Annabelle crumbled into dust. She had been mistaken. No man in love would treat a lady so.

She knelt down beside Annabelle and gathered her into her arms. "There, my child," she said. "Of what use is my old reputation. Men are beasts! Animals! I shall protect you."

"There is nothing you can do," said Annabelle quietly. "I must marry him and save your reputation."

Miss Davenant felt her faith in God waver. Had she not prayed long and hard for guidance? And then, as she held Annabelle, a great idea came into her head.

"Listen," she said urgently, "I think I might be able to hit on a way that would save my reputation and yours and Darkwood's. Now if that comes to pass, would you be happy to be free of him?"

"Oh, yes," sobbed Annabelle. "For that man is a devil. He will take away my soul."

"Then dry your eyes and leave it to me," said Miss Davenant.

Annabelle smiled weakly, but she really did not see what Miss Davenant could do with the town buzzing with such scandalous gossip.

Miss Davenant, despite her newfound comfort, had never forgotten her impoverished friends, a clique of poor relations with whom she often took tea. They pooled their resources, each bringing such little treats to the communal tea table which they could afford. A visit of one of them to a grand relation meant extra food, for each would return from some stately home with a bag full of filched goodies; although no one had the same enterprise and courage as the ancient Miss Primms, second cousin to the Duchess of Berkshire, who returned from one visit to the ducal home with a supply of the best beeswax candles, which she had proceeded to distribute among her friends.

To a startled audience, Miss Davenant outlined the plight of Annabelle Carruthers. "And such a sweet child and so *caring*," she finished. "We must do what we can to help her."

"How?" demanded Miss Primms.

"Like this," said Miss Davenant. "Now, we are supposed to wait until our grand relatives remember our existence and summon us, are we not? But one little visit by each of us to some tea gathering tomorrow would do the trick. I think they will forgive us one visit. I cannot visit Darkwood, but I can visit my cousin, Lady Fremley. Wait until the subject of Annabelle Carruthers comes up or make sure yourself it comes up and say airily you do not know what all the fuss is about for Miss Davenant was resident in the earl's town house while Mrs. Carruthers nursed him. And if you all do your job well, then I shall present each of you out of my allowance with free coals and tea during the winter."

There was a vigorous nodding of gray and white heads. Coals! And tea! The two dearest comforts of a poor old age.

Matilda, Duchess of Hadshire, sat miserably in a corner of Lady Trompington's drawing room. She loathed Lady Trompington, but the duke often chose whom she should visit. Her loathing was made more acute by the relish with which Lady Trompington savored Annabelle Carruthers's downfall.

"Cannot we talk about something else?" demanded Matilda, while mentally damning that treacherous little gossip, Cressida Knight.

But then the poor relation in the corner spoke up. She was a Miss George, an ancient relative of the Trompingtons. Lady Trompington was annoyed that the old quiz should have chosen to invade one of her afternoons. Miss George was usually only taken out and dusted around Christmas. "Such a silly bunch of lies," said Miss George, "and so damaging to poor Miss Davenant's reputation. Lady Kitson should take the birch to that niece of hers and so I shall tell her."

"She told her aunt which was most proper of her so to do," said Lady Trompington, looking down her nose. She wished she had stayed in the country and had only come to town in the hope of seeing that divine Mr. Temple again, but there had been no sign of him.

"Oh, yes, yes," cackled Miss George, "but she forgot to say that Miss Davenant was also in residence."

To Miss George's utter amazement, the beautiful Duchess of Hadshire said, "But of course. I thought everyone knew that. Only very common people are going to take the word of a vicar's daughter. What does Darkwood say himself?"

"Lady Clairmont says he spoke not a word in his defense," said Lady Trompington, "and I have not seen him this age."

"Why should Darkwood say a word in his de-

fense?" said Matilda, doing a deliberate imitation
of her husband at his worst. "He would not stoop
so low. Of course, Lady Clairmont likes to keep it
quiet, but I happen to know that her third cousin
married an ironmaster."

"No!" chorused the ladies in delighted horror.

"So why should Darkwood waste time justifying
his actions to such as she?"

Miss George sat back bemused. Free coal and tea
and she had hardly said a word. The Duchess of
Hadshire had taken the matter out of her hands.

The Duchess of Berkshire was hoping for a visit
from her latest lover. Instead, to her horror, she
received a call from that elderly ancient relative,
Miss Primms. But family duty was family duty. She
produced wine and cakes and settled down to be
thoroughly bored.

But she sat up in amazement as Miss Primms
started to outline Annabelle Carruthers's innocence.
Lady Clairmont had refused to tell the duchess the
name of her dressmaker, and the duchess had not
forgiven her. Also Lady Clairmont set herself up as
an arbiter of fashion and held sway over the sa-
loons of London society. The thought of bringing
her down a peg was delicious. She pressed more
cakes on Miss Primms, and Miss Primms embroidered a good deal but kept to the salient fact that
Miss Davenant had been in residence in Darkwood's house when Mrs. Carruthers was there. Miss
Primms finally became tired. There was a large
plum cake standing as yet uncut on a crystal tazza
on the table.

"Good heavens! Is that someone outside the
door?" she cried.

The duchess recollected her lover and ran to have a look while Miss Primms scooped the whole plum cake into a reticule the size of a coal sack.

The duchess's lover did not call but she did not miss him. She hurriedly dressed to go out. Gossip was more exciting than love any day.

Lady Kitson sent for her niece after she came in from making calls. Normally placid, she looked flurried and upset. "Come and sit by me, Cressida, and tell me child, did you not inform me Annabelle Carruthers was in residence in the Earl of Darkwood's house when he had the fever?"

"Yes, Aunt, and, oh, you *promised* me you would not breathe a word."

"Yes, yes, but listen. Did you tell me that aunt of the earl's, Miss Davenant, was there at the same time?"

In one blinding moment, Cressida saw a way of repairing the damage her gossip had done. "Oh, I knew *that*," she said.

"But," said Lady Kitson faintly, "do you not see that alters the whole scene? If Miss Davenant was there at the same time as Annabelle Carruthers, then there is no scandal."

"I am only a country mouse," said Cressida meekly, "and do not know the ways of the world."

"Goodness, I must fly to Lady Clairmont and apologize and explain. My memory! Are you *sure* you told me about Miss Davenant?"

"Oh, yes, Aunt," said Cressida who firmly believed that lies were all right if the end justified the means.

Once more the Earl of Darkwood was summoned to Lady Clairmont's presence, but this time he refused to go. He judged she simply wanted to read him a lecture. That evening, he attended the opera. The Clairmonts were in their box. To his amazement, Lady Clairmont quite definitely waved to him. Unlike most of the audience, who preferred to study each other, he turned his attention to the performance and happily forgot the existence of the Clairmonts.

At the first interval he was about to rise and go and visit some friends in the neighboring boxes when he received a call from Sir Edward Clairmont.

"My dear fellow," oozed Sir Edward, "such a childish misunderstanding."

The earl, who had been about to brush past him and go on his way, hesitated and raised his thin eyebrows. "Misunderstanding?"

"Yes, yes, that stupid Kitson woman, saying that Mrs. Carruthers had been alone with you in your town house when you had the fever, and now it appears that everyone knew your aunt was in residence as well."

"Everyone?" asked the earl, concealing his surprise.

"Yes, Miss Davenant herself has been most incensed on the subject. My poor wife is in such distress, and Rosamund has quite ruined her pretty eyes with weeping. Do come with me and tell my wife you forgive her."

Bemused, the earl followed Sir Edward to his box. He patiently endured Lady Clairmont's apologies while all the while his mind raced. He had that special license in his pocket. In some miraculous way it appeared his aunt had managed to persuade London society that she had been chaperon to Mrs. Carruthers at every step of the way.

Rosamund threw him a languishing look. Instead of a feeling of freedom, he irrationally felt trapped. He could feel his recent happiness ebbing away.

He did not return to his box after the interval, but left the theater, his interest in the opera gone. He sent his carriage home, saying he preferred to walk.

The air was cold and smoky, and frost sparkled on the cobbled streets. How miserable that last bout of fever had been, he thought as he strode along. And what had happened to the house and servants? Barnstable had said no one could manage servants like Mrs. Carruthers. But she had brought something to his home apart from order and cleanliness, a freshness, a sweetness, a comfort.

He tried to think of Rosamund and found suddenly he could not bear the idea of being shackled to a silly little girl for life, no matter how distinguished her name or large her dowry.

He could always accept the continuing life of a bachelor, sparring at Gentleman Jackson's boxing saloon and going to prize fights and curricle races. On either side of him stood the silent and shuttered shops. He would no doubt settle down into middle age, sedately buying his groceries from Fortnum and Mason, his coal from Findlater's, his drugs from John Bell, his soda water from J. Schweppe & Co. of Berners Street, his snuff from Mr. Fribourg, his silver from Rundell and Bridge, his hats from Lock's, his boots from Hoby's, his newspapers from Mudie's, his books from Hatchard of Piccadilly, and his confectionery from Gunter's. He was rich and could command the best of everything . . . except, said a mocking voice in his head, love and affection and a pair of warm lips and a vulnerable and pliant body that made his senses race.

He put his hand in his pocket and felt the stiff paper of the special license. His steps took him toward Clarence Square. He stood outside the house and looked up. He had treated her badly, mauled her instead of wooing her. All his pampered life, he had taken what he wanted. He had enjoyed the army almost up until Waterloo when he suddenly found himself sick of carnage and bloodshed.

There was a light burning in one of the bedrooms. Was it Annabelle? Had he worried and frightened her so much with his bullying that she was lying awake?

It took a great effort not to go over and hammer on the door and demand to see her. She did not have to marry him now. There was no scandal. She was free to either marry again or to take up that dressmaking career. He thought of her married and could not bear it. He thought of her sitting in some cold attic slaving over dresses and pelisses, ruining her looks and eyesight, and found he could not bear that either.

It broke on him that any prospect of a future without Annabelle Carruthers was a desert. He turned and walked toward his home, wondering what to do.

Annabelle and Miss Davenant found out next day about their restoration to the ranks of the respectable. They received an interesting number of callers. Lady Kitson came bringing Cressida and apologized most warmly. No sooner had she gone than Matilda arrived, braving her husband's anger, to say how some elderly female had told everyone that Miss Davenant had been resident at the earl's town house while Annabelle was there, and Matilda had seen the opportunity of clearing Annabelle's name and had jumped at it. Miss Davenant revealed how she had engineered it, and Annabelle laughed and said she must have a party and invite all Miss Davenant's elderly friends to it. And then, while Matilda was still there, Emma, Comtesse Saint Juste arrived, looking glowing and beautiful.

She demanded to be told the whole story and listened amazed to Annabelle's adventures.

"So you do not need to marry your earl," said Emma, "and we three ladies are together again."

"Except," said Matilda, "that you, Emma, are married to the love of your life. Annabelle is a widow and free, and only I am still in chains."

She began to press Emma for details of her marriage and travels and neither Emma nor Matilda noticed a shadow had fallen across Annabelle's face.

It was that word "free." How beautiful it should sound, how glad she had been at first when she had learned that there was no reason now for the earl to have to marry her. She would not admit that she was in love with him. But she sadly admitted that she was bewitched by him, that she could still feel the imprint of his lips and the strength of his arms.

Downstairs the earl waited impatiently. He had been informed that Mrs. Carruthers had callers, but he did not want to see her again while anyone else was in the room.

He will no doubt call soon, thought Annabelle sadly, and tell me in that stiff and severe way that I have nothing to fear, and then he will go off and propose marriage to Rosamund Clairmont. I *hate*

Rosamund Clairmont. But would it not be splendid if, instead, he came into the room and dropped down before me on one knee and said, "Annabelle, I love you and want to marry you."

"And you are looking radiant, Annabelle," she realized Emma was saying. "This Darkwood is supposed to be a rake, but you must admit he has proved very kind."

"Oh, yes," fluted Miss Davenant, "but he can be brutal. Show them what he did to you, Mrs. Carruthers."

"I beg your pardon?" Annabelle looked bewildered.

"Where he tried to strangle you," said Miss Davenant eagerly. Annabelle was wearing her hair swept up on one side of her head and hanging in loose tresses on the other to cover the bruise on her neck. Before she could guess what Miss Davenant planned to do, that lady lifted her heavy tresses and pointed triumphantly to the bruise.

"Fie, for shame, Annabelle," said Emma and began to laugh. "Is it like that? Is there to be a marriage after all?"

"What do you mean?" demanded Matilda while Miss Davenant looked bewildered. Matilda had slept with her husband two times since their marriage, and it had been a cold, clinical affair each time. Marks of passion were unknown to her.

"Come with me," said Emma, still laughing. "I shall call on you very soon, Annabelle."

"What could she have meant?" demanded Miss Davenant.

Annabelle blushed, but was saved from replying by the arrival of the Earl of Darkwood.

"Please leave us, Miss Davenant," said the earl.

"Oh, no," said that lady stoutly. "For you are not to lay hands on her again."

"My dear aunt . . ."

"Yes, see where you tried to strangle her?"

"It is all right," said Annabelle, blushing harder. "I actually struck my neck on a corner of the mantelpiece and forgot to tell you."

"But why did the Comtesse Saint Juste laugh like that?"

"She knows me of old and knows I am very clumsy."

"Well . . ." Miss Davenant edged to the doorway.

"And shut the door behind you," said the earl pleasantly.

Miss Davenant went reluctantly. She was about to listen at the door as usual when she heard a screaming altercation from the hall. Two housemaids were squabbling and pulling each other's caps. She gave a cluck of irritation and went down to deal with the matter.

"I have a special license in my pocket," said the earl, "but it appears the damage has been repaired and there is no need for it."

"You must be very relieved," said Annabelle. "It appears Miss Davenant has saved the day for us by insisting she was with me all along."

"I am also come to apologize for my rough handling of you."

"Your apology is accepted," said Annabelle bleakly. "No man surely likes the idea of being trapped into an unwelcome marriage."

She was sitting in a small gilt chair by the window, the soft muslin folds of a lilac gown edged with gray showing the lines of her body. She pleated a fold of the muslin between her fingers and wished he would go away and leave her alone. So much for dreams. This haughty earl would never stoop to ask such as she to marry him.

And then she realized he was dropping to one knee in front of her. He took her hand in his, his green eyes looking deep into her own.

"Mrs. Carruthers . . . Annabelle," he said. "Last night when I received the intelligence that I was a free man, I felt quite miserable. I kept remembering all sorts of things, your voice when you read to me, your cool hand on my brow, the way there are fiery little lights in your brown hair when the sunlight falls on it, your grace and beauty and courage, and the infinite sweetness of your lips. I would consider myself the happiest of men if you would allow me the very great honor to care for you the rest of my life."

"As your mistress?"

"As my wife. As my dearest love."

She put her hands on his shoulders and smiled at him, feeling the years of misery and fear roll away.

"Yes," she said simply. "I will marry you and be your wife."

He stood up and drew her to her feet and folded her in his arms and kissed her gently on the mouth.

Miss Davenant waited at her post outside the door to which she had returned after dealing with the housemaids. She could not hear a word from inside. The silence was unnerving her.

Plucking up her courage, she gently opened the door. The earl and Annabelle were wrapped in each others arms. They were deaf and blind to anything else but each other.

Miss Davenant softly closed the door again and leaned againt the panels.

"Thank God," she said. "Oh, thank God!"

Matilda, Duchess of Hadshire, considered herself the most fortunate of women. She had not told her husband of the invitation to Annabelle's wedding, hoping against hope that he would choose that day to be absent from London. She could not believe her luck when the chilly duke announced his plans to travel to Paris to buy a new cloth for his waistcoats. Right up until the last minute, she feared he might command her to accompany him, but he left taking Rougement with him.

On the morning of Annabelle's wedding, Matilda dressed in her finest and then crept down the stairs to let herself quietly out of the house. If one servant saw her leave, then he would report her to the house steward, who would have her followed. It was very lowering to be a duchess and have to arrive at a fashionable wedding in a hack, but the pleasure at being free of the duke and being able to see Annabelle married outweighed any unfashionable discomforts.

The wedding was in St. Catherine's Church in Westminster under the shadow of the Abbey. It was to be a quiet wedding, but there already seemed to be quite a large number of people gathered including a party of elderly females. The grateful Annabelle had invited all Miss Davenant's friends. Cressida was there, overcome with gratitude at having been chosen to be maid of honor along with the Comtesse Saint Juste. Lady Trompington was in attendance, looking as if she were hating every minute of it. She had hoped up until the last minute that it would all prove to be a bad dream and that the earl would come to his senses and marry

Rosamund. But Rosamund had been taken off to the country by her furious parents as soon as the wedding had been announced.

Matilda found herself very affected by the ceremony. She could not help remembering her own wedding and of how, although she did not love the duke, she had hoped, oh so much, that love would come. Although of stern character, she found she was weeping like a child as the bells finally rang out and Annabelle, glowing and radiant in white Brussels lace and pearls, came down the aisle on the arm of her husband.

The wedding breakfast was held at Clarence Square, the elderly ladies with their huge reticules thieving goodies happily right, left and center, although no one could match Miss Primms, who helped herself to coals from the scuttle as well just in case Miss Davenant forgot her promise.

The married couple were to spend their wedding night in a posting house on the Dover road as the earl was taking Annabelle to Paris for their honeymoon. They all crowded out into the square to send the happy couple on their way. Cressida was bursting with pride, quite convinced she had engineered the whole thing, and was to embroider that story in the years to come so that her husband, a gentleman still waiting in the wings of her life, was to become heartily tired of it.

Emma and Matilda clutched each other as the carriage moved out of the square, Emma because she herself was so happy and Matilda because she could not bear to leave this joyful scene and return to her own bitter life. Miss Davenant was annoyed because the rice they had had ready to throw at the happy couple had disappeared and she guessed, correctly, that it was reposing in one of her old friends' reticules.

Miss Davenant was, however, too happy to complain. She had expected to be on her own again, but the earl had suggested she choose one of her friends to live with her, and she looked forward to a tranquil well-fed life.

But inside the carriage, Annabelle did not look like a bride anymore. She looked like a frightened girl. She kept remembering those terrible cyprians in the earl's hall and wondered nervously what would be expected of her in the marriage bed.

The earl stole a look at his wife's downcast features and gave a little laugh. He pulled down the blinds of the coach and jerked her into his arms and began to kiss her passionately. "You have nothing to fear," he said between kisses. "Do you think I would hurt you or do naught but bring you pleasure?"

His new countess kissed him back with rising passion, her fears allayed.

All the hopes of love she thought she had lost were back again. Up on the roof, the coachman blew his horn, and the coach picked up speed and bowled down the chalky road that led to Dover while the earl and Annabelle lay locked in each other's arms and looked forward to the night to come.